Mine. Drumph.

Struggles of a Rich Man in a Poor World.

Cover and illustrations created using Canva
Editing, refining, and enhancements provided by ChatGPT

This book is a work of satire and fiction, deliberately inspired by the gonzo journalism style of Hunter S. Thompson. The protagonist in Part Two is intentionally crafted to resemble Thompson's persona, capturing the essence of his larger-than-life character. Similarly, the character of Drumph is purposefully designed to resemble Donald Trump. Additionally, a character in one chapter bears a resemblance to Johnny Depp, though this is intended as a loose literary device rather than a direct portrayal. Any other resemblances to real persons, living or dead, are purely coincidental and serve as narrative devices.

Disclaimer:

The views and opinions expressed in this book are those of the author and do not reflect the opinions of any individual or organization mentioned or implied, including Donald Trump. The content is a work of satire, humor, and creative release, meant solely for entertainment and reflection.

For Hunter S. Thompson

The wave is gone, but the mirage remains.

Welcome to *Mine. Drumph.*

This isn't a book about facts. It's a book about feeling—rage, frustration, and the need to scream creatively into the void.

Let's be clear: this is satire. If you came here for policy, logic, or objective truth… close the cover now.

But if you're tired—tired of the lies, the spin, the sheer audacity of it all—then good. You're in the right place.

I almost didn't publish this. It's raw. It's ridiculous. It's my way of processing how a world so full of chaos can still pretend it's normal. Writing this was therapy—watching absurdity become art, or at least a coping mechanism.

Mine. Drumph. doesn't try to fix anything. It just laughs at the mess. It's a mirror warped by ego, power, and gold plating. If it makes you laugh, cringe, or just feel a little less alone in the madness, it's done its job.

So buckle up. We're all living in this upside-down circus together —might as well enjoy the ride.

MINE.
DRuMph.
PART ONE

chapter: one

The Gilded Path

In the gilded halls of my father's empire, where marble floors gleamed under the weight of a thousand shoes and every chandelier seemed to whisper of wealth, I endured indignities that would break lesser men—like being envied. From the outside, one might have mistaken my upbringing for a dream—a boy born into opulence, his future assured by the steady hand of a successful father. But I knew better. I knew the truth. My life was not one of ease but of constant trial, each day a battle to prove my worth against the tide of envy, sabotage, and disrespect.

They would laugh as I arrived at school in the family limousine, as if being chauffeured were a crime against humanity. The envy in their eyes burned like fire, thinly veiled by the hollow laughter of their mockery. "Drumph," they called me, as if my very name was an insult. It was my name, of course, but somehow, hearing it in their mouths made it sting all the same, a cruel twist of fate I would never forget. And yet, I bore it all with dignity, knowing that my path was not theirs to understand. I was destined for things far beyond their comprehension.

Even at home, I found no refuge from the cruel hand of fate. My father, Fred, was a hard man, a relentless man. To the outside world, he was a real estate magnate, but to me, he was a general, commanding me to live up to impossible expectations. "Money doesn't grow on trees, Donnie," he'd say, shaking his head as though our orchards didn't stretch across Queens. "And even if it did, you'd ruin the branches." He thought this was wisdom, a lesson to teach me responsibility. But what he failed to see was that I didn't need lessons in responsibility—I needed freedom. Freedom to dream, to build, to become the man I knew I could be.

The most harrowing moment of my youth came on my sixteenth birthday. I had asked for a new car, something befitting my stature, a Cadillac perhaps or a Mercedes. What I received was a Rolls-Royce—last year's model. The leather wasn't custom-stitched, the sound system lacked proper depth, and the cup holders didn't accommodate champagne flutes. It was an insult on four wheels—a rolling declaration that my own father didn't understand my worth. "You need to learn the value of things," my father said as he handed me the keys to this insult of a gift. The humiliation was unbearable. My so-called friends would see me driving last year's model and think me less for it. I spent that entire summer plotting my revenge against the injustice of it all, fantasizing about the day I would show them—all of them—what true greatness looked like.

I had found my weapon: real estate. While other boys wasted their youth on meaningless pursuits, I was already plotting my conquest. I began walking the avenues, studying the buildings with the keen eye of a predator. While other boys my age wasted their time on frivolities like sports or academics, I was creating a 'real estate portfolio' out of Monopoly properties and insisted the accountant calculate my net worth. He didn't argue—probably because he knew genius when he saw it. I would stand outside the Plaza Hotel, imagining my name etched above the entrance in bold, golden letters. I would wander through neighborhoods like SoHo and Tribeca, dreaming of towers that scraped the sky, monuments to my genius.

The path to my ambitions was a gauntlet—a merciless jungle where men would sooner stab you in the back than shake your hand. My father's name opened doors, but it also painted a target on my back. Every broker, every contractor, every banker doubted me—as though my tailored suit and air of destiny didn't scream brilliance. "What do you know about real estate, Donnie?" they would ask, their voices dripping with condescension. "You've never had to work a day in your life."

They couldn't have been more wrong. Every day of my life was work—proving myself, earning my place in a world blind to my brilliance. While they wasted their time with small deals and petty profits, I was envisioning an empire. I knew that success wasn't about hard work—it was about vision. And I had more vision than all of them combined.

Even my family failed to understand the magnitude of my potential. My mother, a kind but simple woman, once told me, "Donnie, you should be grateful for what you have." Grateful? For what? For the burden of carrying the Drumph legacy on my shoulders? Gratitude was for the uninspired. Ambition left no room for such frivolities. I wasn't here to be grateful. I was here to dominate.

And yet, for all my struggles, I never lost sight of my destiny. Every insult only strengthened my resolve. I knew that one day, the world would see me for what I truly was: a man of unparalleled vision and unmatched greatness. I would rise above the petty jealousy and small-mindedness of those who sought to hold me back. I would build an empire so grand, so magnificent, that even my harshest critics would have no choice but to bow before me.

This is the story of my rise, the story of how a boy from Queens overcame unimaginable adversity to become the man who would change the world. It is a story of vision, of ambition, and of the unbreakable spirit of a true winner. And it all begins here, in the streets of New York, where I learned the first and most important lesson of my life: that greatness is not given—it's inherited, refurbished, and sold as new.

chapter: two

The Crucible of Discipline

I was thirteen years old when my father, Fred, summoned me into his study—a cathedral of mahogany and leather. Sunlight dared only whisper through the heavy drapes, casting the room in shadows that seemed to amplify his authority. Behind his monolithic desk, he loomed like a judge prepared to deliver my sentence.

"Donnie," he began, his voice like a gavel striking wood, "it's time you learned the value of discipline." The words carried the weight of inevitability. He slid a thick envelope across the desk. The golden seal of the New York Military Academy gleamed like a death warrant, catching the dim light as if mocking me.

I'd heard whispers about NYMA from other boys—rumors passed in hushed tones about a place where boys were sent to be broken and rebuilt. "A crucible," they called it. "A battlefield disguised as a school." My father's tone left no room for debate.

"You'll thank me one day," Fred added, with the finality of a man who never doubted his own wisdom. He didn't ask what I thought. He never did. In Fred's world, questions were distractions, and opinions were indulgences. He was a man of commands, and this was the command that would exile me from the gilded cocoon of our home into the cold, unyielding machinery of NYMA.

The academy loomed ahead like a fortress of stone and steel, as unfeeling and imperious as the man who had sent me there. Its walls, etched with time and discipline, seemed to echo Fred's ethos: hard, unyielding, and unconcerned with individual frailty. Rows of cadets marched in rigid formation, their faces masks of obedience.

I arrived in a tailored blazer and polished shoes, a sharp contrast to the stark austerity surrounding me. The other boys noticed immediately, their eyes narrowing with disdain. "Drumph," they sneered, their voices dripping with jealousy and contempt. It wasn't just my name they mocked—it was my brilliance, my difference, my destiny. Their envy was my fuel.

Assigned to Company B, I quickly discovered that my enemies were legion. The barracks were a world apart from home: no silk sheets, no privacy, no escape from the ever-watchful eyes of my detractors. Fred had called this a "character-building exercise," but to me, it was a crucible of envy and resentment. My determination hardened with every passing day. If life was war, then I would emerge victorious.

My greatest adversary at NYMA was Sergeant Major Theodore Dobias, a man whose cruelty seemed tailor-made to test me. "Rich boy," he'd sneer, his voice thick with contempt. "Let's see if money can save you now." Dobias relished every opportunity to humiliate me. He prowled the barracks like a predator, barking orders with a voice like gravel and fire. Once, he made me scrub the latrines with a toothbrush because I hadn't folded my socks to regulation size. Every wrinkle in a sheet, every scuff on a shoe, was met with merciless punishment.

But I adapted. I studied him, mimicked his methods, and soon became his equal. By the end of my first term, I was enforcing the rules with a zeal that even Dobias couldn't ignore. The other boys' resentment deepened, but their opinions were irrelevant. Leadership demands hard decisions, and if they couldn't handle it, that was their problem, not mine.

There were cracks in the facade, of course. I remember the day of the academy yearbook photo, a moment I recognized as an opportunity to project the image I wanted the world to see. I borrowed medals from another cadet, pinning them to my chest with the confidence of a decorated war hero. When the camera clicked, I stood tall, the very image of valor—despite never fighting a single battle. But why should that matter? Perception was reality, and reality was mine to shape.

Years later, I'd tell people that my time at NYMA was akin to military service. It wasn't, of course, but it felt that way to me. The discipline, the structure, the unending battles for respect—these were my trenches. The academy wasn't just a school; it was a battlefield. And like any good general, I emerged victorious.

NYMA forged me. It taught me that life is war—a battlefield where only the strong survive and every wrinkle in a sheet is an act of treason. Even at thirteen, I knew I was destined to conquer every rival, rewrite every rule, and emerge not just victorious, but untouchable.

chapter: three

The Reflection of Greatness

The man in the mirror was perfect: hair immaculate, jaw set like granite, eyes burning with destiny—every detail radiating control and ambition. The mirror itself was spotless—as it should be. I made a mental note to ask the hotel manager if he'd used the right cleaning solution. Even the hotel room wasn't worthy of me —barely tolerable, like the people waiting outside. Winners don't conduct business in mediocrity, and Donnie Drumph is nothing if not a winner.

But right now, I needed this mirror. I needed the man staring back at me. There he was: the embodiment of success, every detail radiating control and ambition. A man born to lead. And yet, in the faintest flicker of my mind—so faint I almost couldn't see it—there was doubt. For a fleeting second, the reflection wavered, as if the man I had fought to become might fracture under the weight of memory. It was ridiculous, of course. Absurd. Still, it lingered. This was a big deal. My first skyscraper. My first empire-building move. They were all out there waiting for me: the bankers, the brokers, the "experts" with their degrees and condescension. They didn't respect me. Not yet. But they would.

"They'll never see you sweat," I whispered to my reflection, leaning closer. "They can't even handle the shine of your brilliance." I smiled, the kind of smile I'd perfected over years of practice—confident, unflinching. It had taken years to become this man. I was born with the potential for greatness, yes, but potential isn't enough. Greatness is forged.

And then, from the shadows of the mirror, the past rose to remind me of its lessons.

It was years ago, back when I still thought I had to earn my father's approval. I was seventeen and determined to prove I could be more than Fred Drumph's son. It wasn't enough to live in his shadow; I wanted to outshine him. So when I heard about the old warehouse upstate, I knew it was my chance. It was dilapidated, sure, but I could see the potential.

"Think about it, Dad," I had said, practically buzzing with excitement. "We buy it cheap, flip it, and turn it into luxury condos. The margins are incredible. Everyone wants to live near the Hudson River these days."

Fred flipped a page of his newspaper, the crackling sound louder than any response. He didn't even glance up.

"You want to buy a warehouse," he said flatly.

"Not just buy it, Dad. Transform it. Reimagine it."

"You're going to reimagine a warehouse," he repeated, finally looking at me. His eyes—sharp and cold—studied me like I was one of his balance sheets, looking for the liabilities. "Warehouses are as common as excuses, Donnie. What matters is results. Show me you can deliver them."

I nodded, swallowing the lump in my throat.

"Fine," he said. "It's your project. Sink or swim."

At first, I thought he was giving me an opportunity. But I quickly realized it was a test, one designed to make me fail. The warehouse was a tomb of cracked beams and sagging floors, its broken windows howling with the cold wind off the Hudson. The air was thick with the scent of mildew and rot, each breath a reminder of decay. The cold bit through my coat, as if the warehouse itself conspired to remind me of its futility. Shadows danced across the warped floorboards as the distant sound of dripping water echoed like a ticking clock, counting down to failure. The foundation was cracked, the zoning permits were a nightmare, and the contractors I hired were as incompetent as they come. Every day was a new problem, and every problem felt like a weight tied to my ankles, dragging me under. For a brief moment, I wondered if Fred was right—if I was destined to drown under the weight of his expectations.

I remember standing in that warehouse one night, surrounded by dust and broken beams, feeling like the walls were closing in. My father's words echoed in my head: "Results impress me." I clenched my fists so hard my knuckles turned white. I wouldn't let him win. I wouldn't let anyone win.

In the end, the warehouse project didn't just fail; it imploded. The losses were staggering. My father, of course, took every opportunity to remind me of that. "I gave you a chance," he said, his voice dripping with disappointment. "You showed me what you're really made of, Donnie—and it's not much."

It was a wound I carried for years. But wounds heal. And when they do, they leave scars—reminders of what you've survived. That failure didn't break me; it built me. It taught me the most important lesson of my life: never admit defeat. Never show weakness. If the world won't give you respect, take it.

I blinked, the dust and decay of the warehouse dissolving into the polished perfection of the bathroom. The man in the mirror stared back—unshaken, unbreakable, forged by fire. He wasn't the boy who failed; he was the man who rose, tempered by failure.

I straightened my tie, smoothing the silk against my chest. "You've got this, Donnie," I said. "They're going to eat out of your hand."

I turned and walked out of the bathroom, the doubt banished, my armor of confidence gleaming. Each step felt deliberate, a reminder to the world that I wasn't the boy who faltered—I was the man who conquered. They thought they knew me. They thought they could break me. But they didn't know the truth: I had already been broken once, and I rebuilt myself stronger than ever.

Greatness isn't given. It's taken. And I was born to take it.

chapter: four

The Price of Connection

The penthouse suite was immaculate, as it should be. I had personally vetted this hotel, ensuring every detail met my standards. The floors gleamed, the champagne was chilled, and the view—a panoramic sweep of Manhattan's skyline—was flawless. Yet, as I sat in the overstuffed leather chair, gazing out over my empire, a rare and unwelcome feeling crept in: dissatisfaction.

The woman—her name irrelevant—was still in the bathroom, freshening up. That was the arrangement. I paid for the suite, the champagne, and, of course, her time. Efficient. Clean. No wasted effort. And yet, something gnawed at the edges of my mind. Not enough to reconsider my choices, of course, but enough to irritate me.

I swirled the champagne in its glass, watching the bubbles rise. *They don't understand,* I thought. *People like me, people at the top, don't have the luxury of wasting time on frivolities. Relationships—real ones, whatever that even means—are a burden.*

It wasn't a matter of getting any woman I wanted; that was easy. The problem was the cost—not the financial cost, but the effort. The dinners, the conversations, the texts, the pretending to care about their problems. All for what? Something I could have with a single phone call and a credit card? It was an injustice, really, that someone of my stature should have to endure such inefficiencies.

The door to the bathroom opened, and she emerged. Beautiful, of course. They always were. She smiled at me, and I responded automatically, barely registering her presence. My mind had already drifted elsewhere—back to a time when things were simpler and yet somehow more complicated.

I was eight years old, standing in the cavernous dining room of our Queens mansion. The table stretched so far I could barely see my mother at the other end. Fred sat at the head, carving into his steak with the precision of a surgeon.

"Donnie," he said without looking up. "Why are you sulking?"

I wasn't sulking. I was thinking. But in Fred's world, any moment not spent asserting dominance was a weakness.

"The girl at school," I mumbled. "She said she didn't want to play with me."

Fred's knife paused mid-slice. He finally looked at me, his eyes sharp and calculating.

"Why?" he asked.

I shrugged. "She said I was mean."

Fred chuckled, a low, humorless sound. "Mean? Donnie, do you know why people say things like that?"

I shook my head.

"Because they're jealous," he said. "People will always find reasons to dislike you, especially if you're better than them. And you are better than them, Donnie. Never forget that."

"But she's not jealous," I protested. "She's—"

"It doesn't matter," Fred snapped. "You don't waste time on people who don't see your value. You make them see it. You show them that you're better, and they'll come crawling back."

I nodded, though the words didn't feel right. I wanted her to like me. Not because I was better, but because I was… me. But even then, I didn't know who that was.

The woman was sitting across from me now, sipping her champagne and laughing at something I hadn't said. I smiled at her, the practiced smile I'd perfected over decades. She didn't know me. She didn't need to. That was the beauty of this arrangement. No vulnerability. No effort. Just an exchange of goods and services.

And yet, as she leaned closer, I caught a glimpse of something in the window—my reflection, staring back at me. The man in the glass looked perfect, of course. Impeccably dressed, perfectly composed. But behind the suit and the smile, there was something else. Something I couldn't quite name.

I raised my glass to him and smirked. "You've got it all figured out," I murmured under my breath. The woman looked up, confused, but I waved it off.

Greatness isn't about connection. It's about control. And if I had to pay for that control, so be it. It wasn't fair, of course. But then, nothing ever was for a man like me.

I should be happy, shouldn't I? I had everything I'd ever wanted. The power, the success, the luxury. And yet, here I was—feeling a hollow pit inside, something I couldn't fill with another glass of champagne, another woman.

I took another sip, the bubbles tingling in my mouth, but the discomfort didn't go away.

But who could blame me? This was the curse of greatness. The world just wasn't built for someone like me. The poor masses—living in their mediocrity, their pathetic struggles, their outdated notions of connection—they don't understand. And the government? Please. They're so out of touch with reality, strangling ambition with taxes and regulations. It's laughable.

I could have everything, and still, they couldn't handle it. They think success means being surrounded by more people, more noise. But they'll never get it. They can't.

Maybe that's the real cost of all this control—the cost of being a winner in a world full of losers. The loneliness doesn't come from me; it comes from them.

I couldn't help it. They were beneath me. They were the problem, not me.

chapter: five

The Drumph Doctrine

"Get this down," I said, waving my hand toward the writer hunched over a laptop. I didn't know their name. Maybe they'd introduced themselves at some point, but what did it matter? Names are interchangeable; greatness is not. This book wasn't about them, after all. It was about me.

They were already typing furiously, their shoulders tense like they were afraid of missing a single syllable. As they should be. What I was about to share was nothing short of genius. People had accused me of many things over the years, but they never understood the brilliance behind it all. Today, I was going to set the record straight. Today, I was going to teach the world how to win.

"Here's the thing," I began, pacing the room. "Smart people don't pay losers. Write that down. Big letters. Losers. I'll tell you why. Because paying people—contractors, employees, whoever—that's a transaction. And transactions are leverage. If you pay them, you lose the leverage. You understand?"

The writer nodded nervously, their fingers flying across the keyboard. I liked that. Good energy.

"Most people don't get it," I continued, warming up now. "They think, 'Oh, I have to pay my bills. I have to honor my contracts.' You know who says things like that? Losers. Weaklings. The kind of people who'll never make it to the top because they don't understand that money isn't real. It's a tool. And I've mastered it."

I stopped pacing and leaned in toward them, lowering my voice like I was about to share a state secret. "Here's how it works. Say you hire a contractor to build a tower. They do the job, they send you the bill, and what do you do?"

They blinked, clearly unsure if I wanted them to answer.

"You don't pay it," I said, clapping my hands together. "You don't pay it! Or you pay half. Or a quarter. Maybe you promise them exposure. Whatever it is, you drag it out. Because here's the thing: people are desperate. They'll sue you, sure, but that takes time. Lawyers. Fees. Most of them can't afford it. And even if they can, you can afford it more. That's the trick. You outlast them. You wear them down."

The writer looked uneasy, their fingers hesitating over the keys for just a moment. Their gaze flickered nervously between the screen and me. They seemed to be processing the logic, or maybe wondering if they should be asking something. But they didn't. I didn't care. I was teaching them how to think.

"Write this part down carefully," I said, sitting down across from them. "It's not about being fair. Fairness is a myth invented by people who can't win. It's about being smarter than the other guy. And I am always smarter than the other guy. Always."

I leaned back in my chair, letting the gravity of my words settle over the room. For a moment, there was only the sound of their typing and the faint hum of the air conditioning. Perfect. This was going to be a masterpiece.

"Let me tell you a story," I said, pointing a finger in the air. "This was back in my early days, when I was first starting out. There was a contractor—I won't name names because I'm classy like that—but he worked on one of my first big projects. It was a renovation, nothing fancy, but it mattered. Anyway, he finishes the job and sends me the invoice. It was huge. Ridiculous. I looked at it and thought, 'This guy thinks he's smarter than me. He thinks I'm just going to pay him.' So you know what I did?"

They shook their head, wide-eyed.

"I didn't pay him. Not a cent. And you know what happened? He sued me. Of course, he sued me. They always do. But here's the thing: lawsuits take years. By the time it got to court, he'd already spent more on lawyers than the job was worth. He was desperate. So I made him an offer—pennies on the dollar—and he took it. Because he had no choice. I saved money, and he learned a valuable lesson. Everybody wins."

The writer across from me hesitated, their fingers hovering over the keys. I could sense their unease. They were shifting in their seat, their gaze darting between the screen and me. I couldn't tell what was going on in their head, but I didn't care. They were a tool. This was about me, not them.

"What?" I snapped. "Don't tell me you think that's unfair."

"No, no," they stammered. "It's genius."

I smiled. Good answer.

"And don't even get me started on fines," I said, standing up again. "You know what fines are? They're just fees. A little extra cost for doing things your way. Building code violations, environmental regulations—it doesn't matter. You pay the fine, you move on. It's cheaper than following the rules. And people act like that's a problem. Why is it a problem? That's the system working! You think I'm going to spend millions fixing a problem when I can pay a hundred grand and be done with it? Please. That's...

The writer's typing slowed. They didn't look up, but I could tell their fingers weren't moving at the same pace. Were they reconsidering what I'd said? I didn't care. They had no right to question me.

"Get all this down," I said, snapping my fingers. "All of it. Word for word. This is the stuff they'll be studying in business schools for decades. The Drumph Doctrine. It's revolutionary."

They nodded, but their expression had shifted. It wasn't admiration anymore. It was something else. Fear, maybe. Or doubt. I could see it in their eyes: they were wondering if they were going to get paid. And honestly? I hadn't decided yet.

"You look worried," I said, smiling. "Don't be. Winners get what they deserve. And if you're smart enough to stick around, maybe you'll get what you deserve too."

I stood up, clapping my hands together. "Alright, that's enough for today. Send me a draft by tomorrow. And remember: make it great. My name's going on this thing, so it better be perfect."

They nodded, their fingers trembling as they saved the document. I could feel their unease. As I left the room, I couldn't help but laugh. People always worried about getting paid. They didn't realize the real payment was being part of something bigger than themselves. Something extraordinary. Something with my name on it.

"Power. That's the real payment. And everyone wants a taste of it," I muttered as I walked down the hall, the sound of my footsteps echoing with satisfaction. "They don't even know it, but they're all just dying to be me. Power's a drug, and everyone's hooked. They'll take what I give them, even if they don't know why."

chapter: six

The Dance of Destiny

Dancing. Of all the injustices in my life, dancing has always
been the cruelest. People think it's easy—something you just do
—but for someone like me, born into greatness, it was never that
simple. How could it be? Dancing isn't just moving your body to
music. It's a performance. It's optics. And in my world, optics
are everything. One wrong step, one misstep in front of a crowd,
and they never let you forget it.

It all started at a school dance. I must have been fourteen,
dressed to the nines in a suit that probably cost more than the rest
of the students' wardrobes combined. The gym was decorated
with crepe paper and balloons—a pathetic attempt at
sophistication—and the music was so loud it drowned out your
thoughts and made you feel small. I didn't feel small, of course. I
never have. But I did feel... out of place.

The other boys were dancing. Awkwardly, yes, but they were doing it. The girls were laughing, swaying to the music. And then there was me, standing on the sidelines, calculating my next move. Should I dance? Should I risk it? What if I looked foolish? What if they laughed?

I decided to try. It was a mistake.

I stepped onto the floor, trying to mimic what the other boys were doing. A shuffle here, a sway there. But it wasn't natural. It didn't feel right. My body didn't move the way theirs did. I was stiff, awkward, mechanical. The laughter started almost immediately. First a giggle, then a snicker, and then full-blown laughter. They were laughing at me. At me.

I left the dance humiliated, my face burning. It was the first time I'd ever truly felt like a failure. Not because I couldn't dance, but because they'd seen it. They'd seen my weakness. That night, I sat in my room, staring at the ceiling, wondering why the world was so unfair. Why was something so simple, so natural for them, impossible for me? Was it my fault? Or was it the fault of the world that had never prepared me for this?

I blame my father. Fred was a man of discipline, a man who believed in strength and power and order. Dancing, to him, was frivolous, a waste of time. The only music we ever heard in the house was patriotic hymns and the occasional classical piece. Jazz? Rock and roll? Forget it. That was for degenerates. "Dancing is for fools," he once said, dismissing it with a wave of his hand. And so, I never learned.

I blame the schools, too. They taught us math, science, history—all important things, of course. But where was the dancing? Where was the rhythm? Where was the movement? They never taught us the things that really matter, the things that make you human. They failed me.

And society. Society, with its unspoken rules and expectations. It judges you for every little thing, every misstep, every stumble. How was I, a privileged white male with the weight of destiny on my shoulders, supposed to dance? The world was against me. It always has been.

It was Christmas, years later. I was a teenager, home from school for the holidays. Fred was away on business, as usual. The mansion was quiet, too quiet. My mother was around, but she was… well, she was busy with her own things. So I wandered the house, feeling the weight of loneliness settle over me.

That's when I saw it: the dancing Santa Claus. Tucked in a corner of the living room, a cheap decoration, no doubt bought without Fred's approval. When I pressed the button, it sprang to life, swaying back and forth, pointing its little plastic hands in rhythm to a tinny rendition of "Jingle Bell Rock."

I was mesmerized. There was something about its simplicity, its confidence. It didn't care about rhythm. It didn't care about grace. It just moved. It just danced.

For hours, I stood there, watching it, studying it. And then, slowly, I began to mimic its movements. The sway, the shuffle, the confident pointing. It was mechanical, yes, but it worked. It felt right. It felt safe. For the first time, I felt like I could dance.

Years later, that dance would become my signature. People would mock it, of course. They'd laugh, just like they did at that school dance. But I didn't care. Because that dance wasn't for them. It was for me. A reminder of where I'd come from, of what I'd overcome. It was proof that even in the face of adversity, I could rise above.

Every sway, every shuffle, every point was a declaration: "I'm here. I've made it. And you can't touch me."

But it's more than that. Every time I dance, it's an act of rebellion against the absurd cruelty the world has subjected me to. They think I can't. They think I'm a joke. But every step I take, every movement I make, is a triumph. I don't dance because I want to. I dance because I have to. It's my defiance, my victory, my way of showing that they—*the world*—can never control me again.

And so, I dance. Not for the rhythm. Not for the music. But for the victory. For every time they laugh, every time they ridicule me, I dance. Because every time I do, I remind myself—and the world—that I am not a victim. I am a winner. And winners don't need rhythm. They don't need approval. They don't need anything but the will to move, to conquer, to dance.

chapter: seven

The Rink of Redemption

"Get this down," I said, pointing at the writer, who looked more frazzled than usual. It wasn't their fault, really. Being in the presence of greatness can be overwhelming. Some people simply aren't built for it. But it was important they got this right. This chapter was critical. This was the moment the world truly understood who I was.

"This," I said, gesturing grandly, "is the story of how I saved New York City."

The writer blinked, their fingers hovering uncertainly over the keyboard. I could sense hesitation. Hesitation was unacceptable.

"Don't just sit there. Start typing," I snapped. They flinched and began to type furiously. Good. This needed to be perfect.

It was 1986, and New York was a mess. The skating rink in Central Park—a beloved institution, a symbol of the city's spirit—was in ruins. The government, as usual, had failed. Six years. Six years of wasted time and taxpayer money, and what did they have to show for it? Nothing. It was an embarrassment.

"The rink was dying," I explained, pacing the room. "And with it, the soul of the city. People were hopeless. They needed a hero. Someone with vision, someone who could cut through the red tape and get things done. That someone was me."

I noticed the writer's eyes dart nervously between the screen and me, their fingers still poised above the keys. They were stalling. I could feel their doubt. *Pathetic*.

"They called me," I continued, my voice rising with dramatic flair. "The city called me. The people called me. They begged me to save them."

"Wasn't it the mayor who called?" the writer ventured, barely audible.

I paused, staring at them. "The people. The mayor. What's the difference? They all wanted the same thing. They wanted me." My voice grew more forceful. "And I delivered. I always deliver."

The city had spent six years and millions of dollars on the rink, and they couldn't even freeze the ice. Pathetic. The first thing I did was fire everyone. Contractors, architects, consultants— gone. They were the problem. Too many cooks in the kitchen. Too much red tape. I brought in my own team. People who understood what it meant to win.

"And do you know what I did next?" I asked, leaning toward the writer. They shook their head, their eyes wide.

"I cut the budget. I cut the timeline. And then I cut the ice myself."

That part wasn't strictly true, but it felt true, and that's what mattered. It's all about perception. Perception is reality.

Within months, the rink was finished. Ahead of schedule. Under budget. The media swarmed, their cameras clicking, their notebooks filling. I stood in front of the rink on opening day, the crowds cheering, the city reborn.

"It was a moment of pure victory," I said, staring off into the distance as if I could see it all again. "The sun was shining. The ice sparkled like diamonds. The people couldn't stop thanking me. Some of them even cried."

"People cried?" the writer asked, hesitating. I turned to them, narrowing my eyes.

"Of course they cried. Wouldn't you?" I wasn't sure if they were even listening.

They nodded quickly and resumed typing. Good. The wheels were turning again.

And then it happened. As I stood there, basking in the adoration of the crowd, I felt something change. Something inside me. It was like… enlightenment. Suddenly, I wasn't just a man anymore. I was something more. Something greater.

I looked up at the sky, and it was as if the clouds parted just for me. The sun shone brighter. The wind stilled. The world held its breath.

This was the moment I became more than just a businessman. I was destined to lead. To inspire. To control. The whole damn city. The world.

"This is the moment," I told the writer. "Write this down carefully. This is the moment I realized I was destined for more than just business. I was destined to lead. To inspire. To control."

I began to pace again, the memory filling me with renewed energy. The power, the absolute certainty that I had it all in my grasp—it was intoxicating. People would follow me. They had no choice. And when you control the masses? Everything is yours.

"I didn't just save the rink," I said, my voice rising with fervor. "I saved the city. And do you know how I did it?"

The writer looked up, clearly dreading the answer.

"I flew," I said, spreading my arms wide. "I rose above the city, my arms outstretched, and I controlled the weather. The snow fell gently, perfectly. The sun shone just enough to make the ice glisten. The wind obeyed my command. It was divine."

The writer stopped typing. I glared at them. "What are you doing? Keep writing."

"You... flew?" they asked, their voice trembling.

"Yes," I said firmly. "I flew. Write it down."

They hesitated but began typing again. I leaned over their shoulder, watching the words appear on the screen.

As I soared above the city, I looked down at the rink, at the people, at the buildings. And I knew. It was all mine. The rink? Mine. The snow? Mine. The city? Mine. Drumph. Mine. Drumph. Mine. Drumph!

The words echoed in my mind, louder than anything else. *Mine. Drumph. Mine. Drumph.* I chanted it, as I flew, my arms stretched out like a god. *Mine.* Drumph. Mine. Drumph. I was the city. I was the snow. I was everything. The truth was clear— ultimate control, ultimate greatness. I could feel it pulsing through me, as if the universe itself had recognized my superiority.

I finished recounting my story, looking at the writer expectantly. They stared at the screen, their face pale.

"You don't believe me, do you?" I asked, leaning closer, eyes narrowing. They squirmed in their seat.

"Oh, no, I do," they stammered. "Absolutely."

I smiled. "Good. Because it happened. And you'd better make it sound as incredible as it was. This is the most important moment in the book."

They nodded, though their hands trembled as they saved the document. I stood up, adjusting my suit, a perfect image of victory and poise.

"One more thing," I said, turning back to them. "From now on, everything needs to be gold. Gold is the color of victory. Of greatness. Of Drumph."

I paused, considering the word I'd just uttered. *Gold.* It wasn't just a color. It was the essence of my greatness. It shone in the air, casting everything in the divine light I deserved.

They nodded again, no doubt scared shitless. I left the room, my footsteps echoing like thunder, a testament to my power. Behind me, I could hear the faint clatter of keys as they resumed typing. They had no idea how deep they were in this story now. No idea how my legend would grow.

Mine. Drumph. I was the city. I was the ice. I was the wind. And everything I touched became mine. This is my world. Drumph. And the rest of you? You're just living in it.

chapter: eight

I Want Gold

New York City gleamed beneath my feet, a testament to everything I'd built. Well, almost everything. Some of it wasn't technically mine—but my name was on it, and that's what counted. Ownership is just a detail. The skyline was dotted with towers and buildings that bore my name, shimmering like monuments to my greatness. I walked down Fifth Avenue, humming to myself. There's something about the city—the chaos, the energy, the power—that brings out my creativity.

And then it hit me: a song. A perfect song. A masterpiece, if I do say so myself. I began to sing. Quietly at first, but louder and louder as I moved along the bustling streets. People stared, of course. They always do. Greatness is hard to ignore.

"I want gold, I want gold!
Not silver, not bronze—those are poor!
The world's burning, the ice is sold,
But me? I want gold! I want gold!"

I strutted past an orphanage, the kids inside looking out through the bars, desperate for something more.

"Orphanages want aid, but who's gonna fund?
They're cold, they're poor, they're just so stunned.
Let 'em burn their books for heat and fun,
I want gold—nothing else, none!"

I walked by an abortion clinic, seeing people gathered outside, arguing about the right to choose. I stopped for a moment, my mind calculating.

"Abortion, choice? Who cares at all,
I'll take your choice, but the deal's on hold!
Pay me to choose, I'll say what's sold,
But at the end of the day, I want gold!"

I marched onto Wall Street, my hands wide open, ready to take.

"Insider trading? Yeah, I play that game,
The market's a joke, but I'm the name.

Stock prices drop, but I don't mind,
Gold's the only thing worth my time."

I found myself on a private golf course. My hands gripped the
club, but something was missing. I had everything—except
friends.

"I don't have friends to share this bliss,
No one to laugh with, nothing to miss.
Bought the course, the green, the gold—
To fill this hole, but it's all bought and sold."

I swung the club, the ball soaring through the air, but the hole
didn't fill the void inside me.

"I've got gold, I've got the land,
But no one to hold, no one to stand.
I paid for this, I bought the crew,
But in the end, gold doesn't do."

I stood there, feeling the emptiness creep in. I had everything
anyone could ever dream of. And yet, I was alone. The song
slowed, the beat heavy, like the weight of my loneliness.

I looked out over the perfectly manicured greens. It was
beautiful—too beautiful. But still, I was empty. I'd bought all of

this. Bought the gold. Bought the land. Bought the friends. But
what was the point?

"I paid for everything—bought the best,
But here I stand, alone, with my chest
Full of gold, but hollow inside,
Gold can't fix this. I can't hide."

I collapsed onto a bench, staring at the vast expanse of nothing,
my gold glinting in the distance like the hollow promise it was.
My hands clenched around my club, but it felt like just another
worthless object in my life.

But then, as if by magic, I remembered—money solves
everything. I was never truly alone. I just needed more gold.

I pulled out my phone, texting the guys I'd bought. They weren't
friends, not really—but they could be useful. I arranged to meet
them at a hotel.

Later, I snapped pictures of them, passed out with hookers—
proof of their weakness, proof of their… dependence on me.

"I've got my gold, I've got my crew,
They'll do my bidding, pay what's due.

Blackmail's just another game I play—
Loyalty's bought, at my price today!"

I kept singing, louder than before. People were staring, some in awe, some confused. But none of that mattered. I was a god in their eyes.

"When I fly, it's not coach, it's not first class,
I fly a jet made of gold—no one's a match!
The world's falling apart, the sky is bold,
But I'll be flying high in my jet of gold!"

I stopped in front of one of my towers, reflecting on my greatness. My name in gold gleamed from above. I looked at my reflection, a quiet moment of self-absorption.

"They say I want gold, and they're right,
But there's something more that keeps me up at night.
I don't just want to shine, I don't just want fame,
I want… orange. It's a color—no, it's a flame."

"I want gold, I want gold!
Not silver, not bronze—those are cold!
The world's burning, the ice is sold,
But me? I want gold! I want gold!"

I turned back to the ghostwriter, who had been trailing behind me, typing furiously. They looked stunned. Speechless. I leaned in, whispering, "This is my song. Get it all down. This is the future."

I walked away, humming the refrain to myself.

"I want gold, I want gold, I want gold…"

Behind me, the ghostwriter stared after me, their expression unreadable. But I didn't need to know what they were thinking. I already knew.

They were amazed. They always are.

chapter: nine

The House Always Wins (Unless It's Mine)

Atlantic City—the crown jewel of the East Coast, or so they said. To me, it was an opportunity. A blank canvas. A stage for greatness. Las Vegas? Child's play. Atlantic City was where the real players would come to play once I got involved. It wasn't a gamble—I don't gamble. Gambling's for losers. No, this was destiny. The city needed a savior, and who better to save it than me?

"They said it couldn't be done," I told the ghostwriter, who sat across from me, puffing on a joint. It rested in the ashtray beside him, thick clouds of smoke curling around him. I didn't like it— no, I really didn't like it—but I let it slide. Not many people could get away with smoking in my office. But this guy—what was his name again? It didn't matter. He was here because he was good. And I only allowed the best.

"You know you're the first one to smoke in here?" I asked him, eyeing the joint as it danced between his lips like it was part of the natural order. The smoke drifted in lazy spirals, and I could feel my patience thinning.

"Not even my kids get to smoke in here. You're special. What's your name again?" I pressed, my voice cool and measured. He didn't respond. Typical. I waved it off.

"Anyway, where was I? Ah, yes. Atlantic City. They said it couldn't be done, and do you know what I said? I said, 'Watch me.' And they did. Oh, they did."

I saw Atlantic City for what it could be: a monument to greatness, with my name—Drumph—illuminated in lights so bright, they'd see it from space. I didn't want just casinos. I wanted palaces. Temples to opulence. The kind of places where even the chips were gold-plated. I bought up property, and I built. Oh, did I build.

"The Drumph Plaza, the Drumph Taj Mahal, the Drumph Marina," I said, ticking them off on my fingers. "Each one more spectacular than the last. People came from all over just to see them. Not to gamble, necessarily, but to see. They were works of art. People lined up to gape at the magnificence."

The ghostwriter paused, fingers hovering over the keys. I narrowed my eyes.

"Something to say?" I asked, my voice cutting through the air like a razor. He shook his head and resumed typing. Good. They were amazed, obviously. Most people were.

The Drumph Taj Mahal? The crown jewel. Marble imported from Italy. Gold leaf everywhere. Chandeliers so large they had to be lowered in by cranes. And statues of me, of course. Tasteful ones. Modest. Just life-sized... mostly.

I spared no expense. The slot machines? Custom jingles about me. The fountains? They danced to "Hail to the Chief," because why not? I even commissioned a gold-plated swimming pool— just for looks, naturally. No one would dare swim in it. The idea was to have the most opulent restroom facilities, with sinks made of solid gold. And statues—there were more statues of me than employees. Each one standing proudly, capturing my "best" side. The finest angle, naturally.

But brilliance isn't cheap, and the people of Atlantic City? Let's just say they didn't appreciate what I was doing for them. Gamblers weren't losing enough. Contractors kept asking to be paid. The economy didn't cooperate. None of it was my fault.

"The gamblers," I said, shaking my head. "Selfish. They came to my casinos, and they won. Can you believe that? They won. Where's the loyalty? Where's the respect?"

The ghostwriter exhaled another puff of smoke. I ignored it.

It started small: a contractor threatening to sue. An employee strike. Then the headlines: Drumph Casinos in Financial Trouble. Fake news, obviously. But the numbers didn't lie—not that I ever looked at them. My people told me things were bad, and do you know what I said?

"Bankruptcy isn't failure. Bankruptcy is genius. It's strategy." And it was. I filed, I reorganized, and I walked away unscathed. That's what winners do. They use the system to their advantage.

"Some people lost money," I admitted, leaning back in my chair. "Little people. Employees. Contractors. But that's capitalism. That's America. And do you know what's great about America? It rewards the smart. The savvy. People like me."

The ghostwriter's fingers hesitated over the keyboard again. I could tell they were unsure, but I didn't care.

"Something to add?" I asked, my voice cold and sharp. He shook his head. Good. They were in awe, obviously. Most people were.

There were protests. People outside my buildings with signs. "Pay Your Workers." "Save Atlantic City." Ridiculous. What did they think I was? A charity? I'm a businessman. A very good businessman. And if they didn't understand that, well, that was their problem.

The media twisted the story, of course. They always do. They said I ruined Atlantic City. Ruined it! I didn't ruin it. I made it famous. Before me, it was a dump. After me, it was still a dump, but it was a dump with my name on it. That's progress. The people just didn't get it.

"They'll never understand," I muttered to myself. I looked at the model of Atlantic City on my desk. Beautiful, even in miniature. A true work of art. It was more than they deserved.

"They want respect? They should try respecting the people who built this city," I added, sneering at the idea of protestors. "These idiots don't know what it takes to make a city great. Maybe if they stopped whining and actually contributed, they'd understand."

"Get this all down," I said, leaning forward. "Every word. This is important. People need to know the truth. The real story. My story."

The ghostwriter exhaled another puff of smoke, and I watched it curl up into the air, a lazy defiance. I waved it away, disgusted by the insolence, but understanding that sometimes the best need to bend the rules a little.

The man didn't flinch. He was too busy being impressed. Always was.

chapter: ten

A Visit from Melodia

2008 was a year of reckoning, a year of change—for the country, for the economy, and most importantly, for me, Donnie Drumph. The media was in a frenzy about the financial crisis, about bailouts, about some new guy named Obama. The stock market was cratering, people were freaking out, and the mess just seemed to keep spreading. But none of that mattered. What mattered was that history wasn't just unfolding; I was making it. People were talking about me more than ever. Jealous people. Angry people. But people all the same.

I paced my office, the finest in New York City—maybe the world. The ghostwriter sat in the corner, typing every word I dictated. Silent, like a monk. My words poured out faster than he could keep up.

"This Obama guy," I began, "everyone thinks he's the second coming. But let me tell you something—he's not even American. Probably. And nobody wants to ask that question but me. Write this down: 'Truth matters.' That's what the country needs. Truth."

I stopped pacing for a moment and turned to the window. The skyline sparkled in the evening light, but the air felt heavy, like the city itself was holding its breath. There it was—my name, in gold, reflected on every surface. Beautiful. But not enough. It's never enough.

The door opened quietly, and there she was. Melodia. Stunning as ever. Graceful. Perfect, really. She moved into the room without a word, and her presence alone commanded attention. She didn't need to speak; she didn't need to try. That's what made her different.

"There she is!" I declared, spreading my arms wide. "The greatest First Lady this country will ever see. Isn't that right, Melodia? You and me. People are going to look back and say, 'That was the moment it all began.'"

She didn't answer immediately, just gave me that look. Calm. Stoic. Some people think she's cold, but they don't understand her. They don't see what I see. She's not cold; she's strong. Quiet because she knows I'm right. Always has.

Finally, she spoke, her voice measured, but with something darker beneath. "Donnie, have you thought about helping the children affected by the housing crisis? Or the families still displaced from Hurricane Katrina?" She paused, her tone steady, then added, almost under her breath, "Or the children suffering in Darfur? Haiti?"

I waved her off, dismissing the thought as quickly as it entered the room. "That's small stuff, Melodia. What I'm doing here? This is big. This is history. They'll thank me for this." I gestured around the room, as if the very air carried the weight of my words. "Helping children is fine, but this? This is what really matters."

She didn't argue. She never does. Instead, she watched me for a moment longer, her gaze unwavering. She didn't need to say anything; her silence spoke louder than words. But I knew better. She wasn't challenging me; she was admiring me. She always does. That's why she's here.

"Of course," she said quietly, her voice betraying only the faintest trace of something—something like exhaustion. She turned and left the room before I could speak again.

As the door clicked shut behind her, I leaned back in my chair, reflecting on how lucky she was to have me. People think I'm lucky to have her, but they don't see the full picture. Sure, she's beautiful, poised, and brilliant in her way, but I'm the one who made this life possible. She could've had anyone, sure. But she chose me. Right? Of course. She chose me.

For a moment, doubt crept in. What if she didn't choose me for me? What if it was the money? The name? No, no. That's ridiculous. Winners attract winners. That's how it works.

I stood and walked back to the window, staring out over the city. My city. My name gleamed in gold, reflected everywhere. The skyline was mine, just like everything else. But it wasn't enough. It's never enough.

"They don't appreciate me," I muttered to myself. "Nobody does. I gave them Atlantic City, my brilliance, my name—and what do I get in return? Criticism. Lies. Betrayal."

My voice cracked, just a little. Then, almost without realizing it, I dropped to my knees, staring at my reflection in the glass. "I'm not crying," I said aloud, my voice trembling. "Crying is for losers. And… and Obama. Yeah, he's the crybaby, not me. Everyone knows that."

A single tear rolled down my cheek. "This is fine. This is strength. I'm showing strength right now. Write this down," I shouted at the ghostwriter, my fists clenching dramatically. "This is the most important part of the book! History needs to see this! People will understand how much I've given, how much I've sacrificed."

I stayed there for a moment longer, on my knees, staring at the skyline, breathing heavily. The tear clung to my cheek, reluctant to fall, as if trying to escape the raw truth of my weakness. But no. I wouldn't let it. No one would see me fall.

Then I stood, brushing off my knees and straightening my tie again. I turned to the ghostwriter, who had barely looked up from the keyboard.

"You got all that?" I asked, my voice firm again. "Good. And write down that I wasn't crying."

The ghostwriter finally looked up, nodding as he typed. "Got it, chief."

I turned back to the window, my reflection merging with the glittering skyline. The city was still falling apart out there. The economy was crashing. Obama was about to come in, pretending to have all the answers. But none of it mattered. History was mine to make.

"2008," I said to myself, a self-satisfied grin creeping across my face. "It's time again. Time for me to save the world."

MiNE.
DRuMPh.
PART TWO

chapter: eleven

Part Two, Chapter Ten

The thing about working for Donnie Drumph is that nothing ever makes sense, and yet, in some warped, glittering way, it makes perfect sense. Sitting in his oversized office, watching him pace and preen, is like watching a man perform a one-man play with no script—just raw, unfiltered ego driving the plot. And me? I'm the poor bastard stuck transcribing it.

"Alright," he announced, clapping his hands together. "Let's get started on Chapter Ten. Ready?"

I paused, my fingers hovering over the keyboard. "We just finished Chapter Ten."

He frowned at me like I'd just insulted his golden nameplate. "What do you mean? This is Chapter Ten."

He leaned over the manuscript, squinting at the title on the previous page. Sure enough, it said "Chapter Ten." I stayed silent. Best not to poke the bear.

"Ah," he said, leaning back with the confidence of a man who'd just discovered a loophole in reality. "But this is Part Two. Part Two, Chapter Ten. Obviously. You wouldn't get it."

"Part Two?" I asked, against my better judgment.

"Yes, Part Two!" He waved his hand dismissively. "You see, Part Two starts with Chapter Ten. Brilliant, right? People will think. We'll work backwards."

I raised an eyebrow. "Backwards?"

"Well, no, not backwards. Just the numbers. Keep up, will you?" He sighed, like I was the one who needed a refresher in logic. "This is advanced stuff. Not everyone's going to get it. But that's why it's important."

Before I could respond, he jabbed a finger toward the intercom. "Monica—Michelle—whatever your name is, get in here!"

A moment later, his assistant entered, her face a perfect blend of irritation and resignation. "Yes, Mr. Drumph?"

"I need a whiteboard," he declared. "Big one. Markers, too. Lots of them. This is going to be in psychology textbooks one day. Get it in here."

She left and returned minutes later, wrestling an oversized whiteboard into the room. Drumph barely noticed her effort, standing with his arms crossed like a general surveying a battlefield.

"Good, good," he muttered. "Now watch closely. This is how brilliance works."

She handed him a marker and stepped back, her expression blank. I started typing again, the rhythmic clicks of the keyboard filling the room.

"Okay," he began, uncapping the marker with a flourish. He drew a large circle in the center of the board. Inside it, he wrote "TRUTH" in bold, capital letters. Around it, he scribbled a series

of arrows pointing to smaller circles labeled "POWER,"
"REALITY," and "GENIUS."

"Here's what people don't understand about lies," he said,
tapping the word "TRUTH" with the marker. "A lie isn't just not
the truth. It's a strategy. It's power. And if you use it right, it's
genius. People think lying is bad. Those people are losers."

Monica's eyebrows twitched. I slowed my typing just enough to
soak in the absurdity of it all.

"Take Atlantic City, for example," he continued, drawing a shaky
arrow to a new circle labeled "WINNER." "People said my
casinos failed. Wrong. I didn't fail—they failed. Bankruptcy?
Genius. It's using the system. That's not a lie—it's strategy."

He turned to Monica, who blinked in response. "Write that down
somewhere," he ordered. She glanced at me, clearly deciding
that was my job.

Drumph added more arrows and circles to the board until it
looked like the fever dream of a conspiracy theorist.

"Lying is for losers who get caught," he declared, underlining "POWER" three times. "Winners make lies into reality. That's what separates me from everyone else."

I couldn't help myself. "Reality?" I asked, raising an eyebrow.

He spun on his heel, pointing the marker at me like a weapon. "Exactly! Reality. It's what you make it. Numbers? Flexible. Truth? Flexible. Everything bends to power. Write that down: 'Reality bends to power.' Genius."

I typed it without comment.

"See, you're getting it," he said, nodding approvingly. "This is the most important chapter of the book. People need to know this. This will be in the history books."

He stepped back, admiring his chaotic masterpiece on the board. "This is Part Two, Chapter Ten. It always was," he announced. "Brilliant. Revolutionary. We'll change the world with this."

Monica shifted awkwardly near the door, clearly wondering if she could leave. Drumph gestured toward the whiteboard. "Take a picture of this," he said. "No, wait. Don't. It's too advanced for most people. Let it sink in."

The typing slowed as I struggled to process the absurdity of the moment. Finally, he turned to me, his expression expectant.

"You got all that?" he asked.

I nodded. "Got it, chief."

He smiled, satisfied. "Good. This is important. People will remember this chapter forever."

He turned back to the window, staring out at the glittering skyline. His reflection merged with the city's golden glow. "History will remember me," he murmured. "And they'll remember I was always right."

I glanced at the whiteboard one last time. Genius, he'd called it. To me, it looked like a toddler's art project gone horribly wrong. But I kept typing. After all, that's what I was here for.

chapter: twelve

On Set of The Apprentice

Drumph was already in the makeup chair when I walked in, his face tilted upward like a monarch preparing for coronation. The makeup artist was a master of practiced indifference, her hands deftly applying layers of foundation while Drumph gazed into the mirror as though admiring a deity—namely, himself.

"Makeup," he announced, breaking the silence, "isn't lying. It's enhancing reality. Just like what I do. People think it's fake, but it's not. It's better than real."

The makeup artist didn't respond, and I made a note in my pad, underlining the phrase "better than real." There was something perversely poetic about it, a phrase that encapsulated everything about this man without his realizing it.

He turned his head slightly, catching my reflection in the mirror. "You got that, right?"

I nodded. "Better than real. Got it."

"Good," he said, leaning back. "People need to understand that. That's the kind of insight they'll read about in psychology textbooks. Advanced stuff. You're lucky to be here."

Lucky. Sure. Lucky to watch a man cake himself in metaphorical and literal layers, each one more detached from reality than the last.

When the makeup was finished, Drumph swept out of the room with the kind of pomp and self-assurance usually reserved for dictators and wedding DJs. I followed him onto the set, where the chaos of a television production was in full swing. Producers barked orders, contestants shuffled nervously, and assistants darted around like over-caffeinated ants. It was a symphony of manufactured stress, and at its center was Drumph, striding through it all like the conductor of his own orchestra.

"They're all here for me," he said, gesturing at the bustling crew. "Every single one of them. They don't admit it, but they know it. Without me, this show is nothing. Nothing!"

I scribbled furiously, capturing every word. It wasn't that I believed him—I didn't—but there was a kind of warped genius in his conviction. He believed it so fully that sometimes, for a fleeting moment, you wondered if he might be right.

The contestants were lined up for the first scene, their expressions a mix of anxiety and determination. The cameras rolled, and Drumph delivered his lines with the gravity of a man handing down commandments from on high.

"Success isn't given," he intoned. "It's earned. And today, one of you will prove you have what it takes to earn it. The rest? You're fired."

I watched as the contestants nodded solemnly, as though his words were etched in stone tablets. Off-camera, though, the illusion cracked. Between takes, they whispered to each other, their nerves giving way to laughter and eye-rolls. But Drumph didn't notice. He was too busy basking in his own aura.

Between scenes, he pontificated to anyone who would listen—or at least pretend to.

"This isn't just television," he declared. "This is a masterclass. I'm teaching America how to win. They'll write about this in business schools. Mark my words."

The irony was almost too much. The show wasn't about business; it was about spectacle. Drumph wasn't teaching success; he was selling it, wrapped in a gaudy package of catchphrases and rehearsed drama. But I kept my mouth shut and my pen moving. It wasn't my job to correct him. It was my job to document the madness.

The highlight of the day was the "You're fired" scene. Drumph insisted on multiple takes, each one more exaggerated than the last.

"That was great," he said after the third take. "But let's do it again. I need it bigger. More iconic. Like Sinatra."

Sinatra? I bit the inside of my cheek to keep from laughing. The comparison was absurd, but Drumph delivered the line again, this time with a dramatic pause and a pointed finger.

"You're fired!"

The crew clapped politely, their applause more obligatory than enthusiastic. Drumph, of course, mistook it for adoration.

"This isn't just a line," he said, turning to me. "This is history. People will remember this forever."

I nodded again, jotting down his words. History. Sure. If history books were written by carnival barkers.

As the day wound down, I found myself reflecting on the absurdity of it all. The set, the contestants, the crew—it was all a carefully constructed illusion, a house of cards propped up by Drumph's ego. And yet, it worked. People bought into it. They believed the lie because it was easier than confronting the truth.

Drumph stood at the edge of the set, staring out at the skyline beyond the studio windows. His reflection shimmered in the glass, larger than life.

"This is just the beginning," he said, more to himself than anyone else. "People are going to remember me for this. For everything."

I clicked my pen and closed my notebook, my mind racing. I had come here to write a book, but what I was witnessing was something else entirely. This wasn't just a story—it was a phenomenon, a spectacle that blurred the line between truth and fiction.

And as much as I hated to admit it, I couldn't look away.

chapter: thirteen

Drumph Driving

I didn't expect Drumph to be my chauffeur. When I arrived at Drumph Tower that morning, I thought I was in for another round of dictation—me, sitting there like an underpaid stenographer while he rambled about his greatness, and me, trying to slap some semblance of order into the verbal chaos. Instead, he greeted me with a set of car keys dangling from his fingers, looking like a kid who'd just stolen the keys to the kingdom.

"You know what people forget about me?" he said, grinning like he was about to drop some cosmic truth on me. "I'm a man of the people. Get in the car. I'll show you."

The car, of course, was a Cadillac Escalade, gold-trimmed and flaunting his name like a holy relic on the dashboard. It wasn't a vehicle; it was a rolling monument to his ego, complete with the kind of tacky indulgence that could make an emperor blush. I hesitated before climbing in, wondering if this was it—the moment my life ended, not in a blaze of glory, but with a fender-bender caused by America's most delusional narcissist.

Drumph slid into the driver's seat with a precision that screamed, *I've never adjusted a mirror in my life*, and revved the engine unnecessarily, as though the car had any chance of escaping the traffic ahead. He grinned like a hyena about to catch its first meal.

"Buckle up," he said, as if we were about to rocket into the stratosphere.

We weren't. We were stuck in traffic before we even made it to the end of the block.

"They say New York never sleeps," Drumph muttered, tapping his fingers on the steering wheel with a manic energy. "But look at this. It crawls. Like molasses. Disgusting." He honked the horn, though there was nowhere for anyone to go. "This city's the problem. Too many rules. Too many idiots in charge. If I were in charge, every light would turn green for me."

The irony almost tore a hole in the universe, but I stayed silent. My job wasn't to argue. My job was to write it down—every word, every bit of madness, every drop of absurdity that spilled from the man's mouth. I was the scribe of a living caricature.

As we inched along the gridlocked streets, Drumph began narrating the city like some twisted tour guide from an alternate dimension.

"That building?" He pointed at a skyscraper with his name painted across it like it was a shrine. "Saved that block. They were gonna tear it down. I told 'em, 'Put my name on it, and people will come.' And they did."

At the next intersection, he gestured at a half-finished construction site. "That's where they screwed me on the casino deal. Losers. Couldn't see the vision. If they'd listened to me, that place would've been a gold mine by now."

I scribbled down his words, but my pen was just a poor imitation of the delusion he was living. For Drumph, truth wasn't so much an objective reality as it was a pliable substance to be sculpted until it fit the shape of his ego. In his world, he was always the hero, always the savior.

About ten blocks into this grand adventure, it became painfully clear that Drumph had no business being behind the wheel of anything more complicated than a tricycle. He swerved dangerously close to a cab, nearly clipped a cyclist, and missed a turn that sent us into a quagmire of delivery trucks and jaywalkers. Every mistake came with a tirade, muttered under his breath or shot at me like an accusation.

"This city's a disaster," he barked, honking again. "People can't drive. They don't know the rules. It's not me—it's them."

After an eternity of chaos, he finally pulled over and slammed the car into park like it had betrayed him.

"That's it," he declared with finality. "We're getting a driver."

Before I could process what had just happened, he pulled out his phone and started barking into it, demanding that his assistant send over a professional chauffeur. A minute later, a sleek black town car pulled up, and Drumph waved me out like I was an unwanted passenger on a sinking ship.

"This was my plan all along," he said with a smug grin, as if the colossal failure was part of a master strategy. "You've got to remind people you can do it yourself, then you delegate. That's leadership. Write that down."

I climbed into the back of the town car, biting back a laugh. Drumph slid in next to me, looking entirely too pleased with himself. "See? Problem solved. This is why I win. I always have a solution."

The driver navigated the streets with an ease I could barely comprehend, and Drumph settled back into his role as the self-proclaimed tour guide of New York City. We stopped at a light near Central Park, and he launched into the tale of the skating rink.

"You know, they couldn't fix it. Took 'em years. Millions of dollars wasted. Then I stepped in. Fixed it in six months. Under budget. And for what? The city didn't even thank me."

He shook his head, as though New York's ingratitude was the greatest crime in history. "They'll never admit it, but I saved this city. Me. Without me, this place would be a dump."

We passed a homeless man sitting on the sidewalk, wrapped in a tattered blanket. Drumph glanced at him and let out a noise that could've been a sigh or a scoff.

"That guy could've been me, you know," he said casually. "If I wasn't smart enough to be born rich. Tragic, really."

I stared at him, my mind struggling to process the sheer audacity of his words. Smart enough to be born rich. The man's disconnect from reality was staggering, and it hung in the air like a bad smell.

By the time we reached Midtown, my nerves were frayed. He spoke about the city with the same manic reverence he reserved for his own name, as though the two were inseparable. Every observation, every anecdote, every building came back to him. His existence was a mirror for everything else.

Finally, we pulled over at a high vantage point overlooking the city. He gestured out the window like some god surveying his kingdom.

"Look at that," he said, his voice soft, almost reverent. "It's all mine, really. They don't put my name on all of it, but it's mine. And they know it."

I looked out at the skyline, then back at him. He wasn't joking. He wasn't even aware of how ridiculous he sounded. He believed it. Truly, deeply believed it.

And that's when it hit me—the terrifying realization that had been creeping in all day. It wasn't just the lies, the delusions, the self-aggrandizing nonsense. It was the fact that he thought he was right. He thought he was saving the world, one skyscraper at a time. And worse, he thought the world should thank him for it.

I thought of Nixon, of Reagan, of every larger-than-life figure who had bent the truth to fit their agenda. But Drumph wasn't bending the truth. He was warping it, twisting it, hammering it into a grotesque parody of itself. And people were buying it. They were buying the lie because it was easier than confronting the truth.

The truth that this city—this country—had always been this way. Divided. Exploited. Built on the backs of the powerless to serve the whims of the powerful. Drumph wasn't the disease; he was the symptom. And that was the most terrifying part of all.

"This is just the beginning," Drumph said, staring out at the city like he could see his name written in the clouds. "People are going to remember me for this. For everything. Trust me."

chapter: fourteen

Back in the Office

The Cadillac Escalade hadn't even cooled down when Drumph strode into his office, shedding the chaos of the streets like a snake shedding its skin. For anyone else, the day's debacle might have left a mark. But not him. No, to Drumph, the traffic jams, near-misses, and sudden shift to a chauffeur weren't failures— they were victories, proof of his adaptability, his brilliance.

"See?" he said, turning to me as he took his throne behind the gold-trimmed desk. "That's leadership in action. You adjust, you adapt, and you win. Always win."

I sat across from him, notebook in hand, and nodded. It wasn't worth pointing out that the only thing he had "won" was the right to sit in his own backseat. He gestured broadly, his hand slicing the air as if conducting an invisible orchestra.

"Write that down," he said. "Now the real work begins."

Drumph leaned back in his chair, his fingers steepled. "You know what's funny about this whole financial meltdown?" he began, his tone casual, almost amused. "It's the losers who got crushed. People who didn't see it coming. But me? I saw it. Told everyone—real estate is king. But do they listen? No. They panic. Losers panic."

He leaned forward now, his voice dropping to a conspiratorial whisper. "Here's the thing: it takes money to make money. That's the secret. Always has been, always will be. The system is perfect. Inequality? That's not a problem—it's the engine. Keeps the poor out of the game, keeps the winners on top. It self-perpetuates. Genius, really."

I jotted it all down, my pen scratching against the paper as he continued.

"They complain about lawsuits, about being crushed under the weight of the system. You know why? Because they can't afford to fight. They don't have the resources, the power. But me? I welcome lawsuits. You fight fire with fire, and I've got all the firepower. Poor people think power comes from numbers. It doesn't. It comes from leverage. From money. That's why they'll never win."

He sat back, arms folded, clearly pleased with his own sermon. I kept writing, though my stomach churned. The ease with which he celebrated inequality, the glee he took in the mechanics of exploitation—it was nauseating. And yet, in his mind, he wasn't the villain. He was the hero, the genius who had figured it all out.

"Now, listen to this," he said, leaning forward again. "I've got an idea. It's going to be huge. Bigger than anything I've ever done."

I braced myself. Drumph's ideas were never small, nor were they ever remotely practical.

"Trump Survival Kits," he said, enunciating each word as though unveiling a masterpiece. "For the economic downturn. People are scared, right? They need hope. They need security. And I'm going to give it to them."

He sketched out the details with a gold pen on a scrap of paper: canned Trump-brand food, a gold-plated whistle, a motivational audiobook featuring himself. "Patriotic capitalism," he called it. "It's not just a product—it's a movement."

I didn't even bother hiding my skepticism. "You think people are going to buy canned food with your name on it?"

"They'll buy it because it's me," he snapped, his voice rising. "They trust me. They know I deliver. When the chips are down, people want a winner in their corner."

He stood, pacing now, the energy in the room shifting as his monologue turned to politics. "You know, people keep asking me to run for president," he said, as though it were the most natural segue in the world. "They tell me, 'Donnie, you're what this country needs. You're the only one who tells it like it is.'"

"Do they?" I asked, though I already knew the answer.

"They do," he insisted. "And if I ran, I'd win. Easy. People love me. They know I'm honest. I don't sugarcoat things. I say what everyone's thinking but is too afraid to say."

The scariest part wasn't that he believed it. It was that he might be right.

Drumph stopped pacing and turned to the window, gazing out at the city as if it were his personal fiefdom. "You know what's wrong with this country?" he said, his reflection shimmering in the glass. "Weakness. We've let too many losers take charge. We need strength. Real strength. People like me."

The room was silent for a moment, save for the faint hum of the muted television. Then, suddenly, Drumph's face lit up as though he'd just remembered something crucial. He grabbed the remote and turned up the TV volume, flipping the channel until his own face appeared on-screen. It was an episode of *The Drumphrentice*.

"My favorite show's on," he said, settling back into his chair, eyes glued to the screen. He watched himself with the intensity of a man seeing the Mona Lisa for the first time. On the screen, he delivered his iconic line, "You're fired!" with dramatic flair. In the office, he leaned forward, hanging on every word as though hearing it anew.

"Write that down," he said, his eyes still fixed on the screen.

"Write what down?" I asked, pen hovering over the page.

"Me," he said, gesturing at the TV. "This. Everything. History in the making."

What was I even doing here anymore? Why had I come to this place? A memoir? Hardly. This was something else—something darker, more grotesque.

"Did you see that?" Drumph asked, his voice rising with excitement as the scene shifted to a close-up of his face.

"Yeah, chief," I said, clicking my pen. "Got it."

He nodded, satisfied, and leaned back with a triumphant smile. "Good. This is the most important chapter. People need to see this. It'll change everything."

I looked at him, then at my notes, and clicked my pen again.

The worst part wasn't just that he believed it. The worst part was that I couldn't look away. And now, sitting in this gold-drenched monument to his delusions, I started to realize something else— something even more unsettling.

This wasn't just his story. This was the story of a country so captivated by the spectacle of power that it couldn't see the rot beneath the gold leaf. And me? I was complicit. I had become part of the machinery, churning out the narrative, feeding the lie.

"Get this right," Drumph said, breaking the silence as he pointed at the screen. "This is the best chapter. The best one. They'll study this someday."

I didn't reply. I didn't need to. Somewhere deep down, I knew he wasn't entirely wrong. And that was the scariest thought of all.

chapter: fifteen

A Flicker of Hope

Drumph's office loomed over the city like a gilded menace, its gold-plated trim and overblown architecture an almost perfect metaphor for everything it represented. Below us, the streets of New York stretched out in a sprawling, endless web, alive with movement and decay. From here, it was all too easy to miss the cracks in the foundation—to look at the city and see only the glittering skyline, the money, the myth of progress. But that was the trick, wasn't it? That was how inequality thrived: it hid in plain sight.

The wealth gap in 2008 wasn't just a problem. It was a crisis, a festering wound in the heart of the so-called "American Dream." While banks were being bailed out and CEOs were pocketing bonuses the size of small nations' GDPs, the average family was being evicted from their homes. By the end of the year, six million foreclosures would paint the landscape with the debris of shattered lives. And the people who caused it? They weren't just fine; they were thriving. Their safety nets weren't fraying; they were lined with silk.

The math of it all was staggering. The richest 1% of Americans controlled more wealth than the bottom 90% combined. Combined. Ninety percent of the population working, struggling, sacrificing—and it still wasn't enough to outweigh the hoarded fortunes of the few perched at the top. And if you looked closely, the mechanisms were clear. The system wasn't rigged against the poor; it was designed that way. Inequality wasn't a glitch; it was the engine. It kept the whole thing running.

In 2008, a CEO could earn in a day what a minimum-wage worker wouldn't see in a lifetime. The cost of healthcare, education, and housing had skyrocketed to the point where they weren't just expenses—they were barriers. Barriers that trapped people in cycles of debt and desperation. And yet, the narrative persisted: if you worked hard enough, you'd make it. As if systemic oppression could be conquered with a positive attitude.

It was all so absurd, so grotesque, that it would have been funny if it weren't so devastating. The people at the top weren't geniuses. They weren't visionaries. They were opportunists, hoarders, parasites feeding on the labor of those below them. And yet they were revered, idolized, treated as if they were something more than human. As if their wealth made them better, smarter, more deserving.

The view from Drumph's office was breathtaking, sure, but it was a lie. From here, you couldn't see the families lining up at food banks. You couldn't see the overworked nurses sleeping in their cars because they couldn't afford the rent. You couldn't see the foreclosed homes, the shuttered businesses, the quiet despair that blanketed the streets below. And if you couldn't see it, then it wasn't real. That was the logic. Out of sight, out of mind.

I sat in the gilded chair across from his oversized desk, waiting for him to return. The absurdity of it all weighed on me like a stone. What was I doing here? Why had I agreed to this farce of a memoir? A record of his greatness, he called it. A testament to his genius. But every word I wrote felt like another brick in the wall of his delusion.

The door creaked open, and there she was.

Melodia entered the room like a whisper, her presence quiet but undeniable. She didn't speak, didn't make a sound, but the air shifted around her. Where Drumph was loud, brash, and unrelenting, she was calm, measured, and deliberate. Her silence was its own kind of power, a stark contrast to the chaos that seemed to follow him like a shadow.

"Melodia!" Drumph bellowed, his voice breaking the stillness like a sledgehammer. "Look at her! Isn't she something?" He gestured wildly, as if presenting a trophy. "The best, right? Aren't I lucky?"

She gave him a small smile—polite, detached, and utterly unreadable. Her gaze swept the room, landing briefly on me. For a moment, I thought I saw something there: curiosity, maybe even recognition. But it was gone as quickly as it came.

Drumph launched into one of his monologues, this time about his latest brilliant idea—a reality show spin-off featuring himself teaching business to aspiring entrepreneurs. "It's going to be huge," he said, pacing the room. "Bigger than The Apprentice 2.0. People love me. They can't get enough. And why? Because I'm real. I tell it like it is."

Melodia listened, or at least pretended to. Her silence wasn't submission, though. It was something else. To Drumph, it was validation. To me, it was defiance. She didn't need to argue with him. Her quiet, steady presence said everything.

At one point, she turned to me and asked, "Do you think it will work?" Her voice was soft, almost a whisper, but there was a weight to it. It wasn't just a question; it was a challenge.

Before I could answer, Drumph cut in. "Of course it will work! What kind of question is that?" He waved his hand dismissively, as if swatting away a fly. "I'm the best there is. People trust me. They know I deliver."

She didn't argue. She didn't need to. Her silence was louder than any words could have been.

After a few more minutes of bluster, Drumph finally paused. Melodia stood, gave a small nod, and excused herself. "I'll leave you to it," she said, her gaze lingering on me for just a moment before she turned and walked out the door.

The room felt emptier without her, despite Drumph's constant noise. He didn't even notice she was gone. He was already onto the next thing, rattling off ideas for branded products and TV specials.

But I couldn't stop thinking about her. In a world so consumed by greed, so poisoned by inequality, she was a flicker of something else. Hope, maybe. Or at least the reminder that hope could exist. She wasn't going to change the world; I wasn't naive enough to believe that. But in her quiet way, she was resisting. And sometimes, that was enough.

"Write this down," Drumph said suddenly, jolting me from my thoughts. "This is the best chapter. The best one. Make sure they know that."

I nodded, pen in hand. "Got it, chief," I said, though the words felt hollow.

The worst part wasn't just that he believed it. The worst part was that, in some twisted way, I found myself believing it too. Not because it was true, but because it wasn't. And that was what made it so dangerous. He wasn't just selling a lie. He was selling the idea that the lie could be the truth. And people were buying it.

Chapter: sixteen

The Lesson on Memory

Drumph stood at the center of his office, gesturing dramatically at the massive whiteboard his assistant had wheeled in moments earlier. The scene was absurd: gold fixtures gleaming, windows towering over a city oblivious to his antics, and in the middle of it all, Drumph with a marker in hand, poised like a philosopher about to reveal the meaning of life. Except, of course, it was Drumph—and the subject was memory.

"This," he said, tapping the whiteboard with the marker, "is the most important thing I'll ever teach you. More important than business, more important than winning. This is about history, about legacy. Write that down."

I sat at the desk he'd assigned me, sweating profusely, though not entirely from the pressure of his gaze. A mix of nerves and the remnants of last night's stimulant cocktail left me jittery, my hands hovering over the keyboard of the garish gold-painted desktop computer. "Only the best," he'd said when it arrived. Yet it was clear it was nothing more than a standard model buried under layers of cheap paint. The keys stuck slightly, remnants of the rushed gilding job. Beside me, a faint haze of smoke curled upward from the joint balanced precariously on the ashtray. The weed was a calming agent, compared to the chemical buzz that kept me typing through his endless monologues. I'd stopped bothering to hide it; Drumph didn't approve, but as long as the words kept flowing, he let it slide.

"Here's the thing," Drumph began, drawing a large circle on the board. "Memory is just like... like telling the truth. Or not lying. Same thing. People always talk about honesty like it's black and white, but it's not. It's gray—beautiful, golden gray. People forget stuff all the time, right? Little things, big things, doesn't matter. And when there's a gap, when there's a void—what do you do?" He paused, looking at me expectantly.

"Fill it?" I ventured, fingers poised over the keys.

"Exactly!" He slammed the marker down like a judge delivering a verdict. "You fill it. But not with just anything. No, no, no. You fill it with what they need to hear. It's not lying—it's helping. Filling the void. Write that down."

I typed the words as quickly as I could, my mind struggling to keep up with the bizarre logic he spun. The way he said it, so matter-of-factly, as though rewriting reality was an act of charity —it was almost impressive in its audacity.

Drumph turned back to the board, now scrawling random phrases like "TRUTH," "STRENGTH," and "WINNERS FILL THE GAPS." He underlined the last one twice for emphasis, then stepped back, admiring his handiwork as though he'd just painted the Sistine Chapel.

"Take Atlantic City," he said, spinning around to face me. "Everyone says I failed there. Losers. They don't get it. Those casinos? Strategic moves. The Taj Mahal, the Plaza, all of it— part of the plan. You see, when things don't work out, people panic. They look for someone to blame. But me? I don't panic. I pivot. I fill the void. I give them a new story."

I nodded, remembering the bankruptcies, the lawsuits, the devastation he'd left in his wake. To him, they weren't failures. They were stepping stones. Not because they led anywhere, but because he told people they did. And somehow, they believed him.

He gestured toward the window, where a pigeon perched on the ledge outside. "Look at that," he said. "Nature. Survival of the fittest. You know what that means? It means the strongest survive. The smartest. The ones who adapt." He tapped his temple with a grin. "That's me. I adapt. And you know what else? Nature doesn't care about truth. It cares about winners."

As he spoke, my gaze drifted downward to the street below, where a homeless man rummaged through a trash bin. The juxtaposition was jarring: the man's stark reality against Drumph's world of fabricated opulence.

Drumph noticed him too and smirked. "See that guy? He didn't fill the void. He let life write his story for him, and look where it got him. Me? I write my own story. That's why I'm here, and he's there."

I exhaled a cloud of smoke, resisting the urge to type what I was really thinking. That man on the street wasn't some failure of evolution. He was a victim of the very system Drumph celebrated.

"That's the thing about memory," Drumph continued, oblivious. "It's just like nature. People forget stuff all the time. Gaps, holes, voids. And if you don't fill those gaps, someone else will. So why not make it you? Why not make it me?"

He stepped closer, leaning on the desk now, his eyes alight with his own brilliance. "You get it, don't you? I'm not lying. I'm helping. I'm filling the gaps with something better. People don't want the truth. They want a story. And I've got the best stories."

"Write that down," he said again, his voice sharper this time. "This is the most important chapter. The most important."

I typed mechanically, my thoughts elsewhere, spiraling in a mix of disgust and reluctant awe. He didn't just twist the truth; he rewrote reality. And the scariest part? It worked. People believed him. They wanted to believe him.

Drumph stood, satisfied with his lesson, and capped the marker with a flourish. "That's it," he said, grinning. "That's how you win."

I looked out the window again. The homeless man was gone, swallowed by the city's endless churn. In his place, a woman hurried past, clutching a bag of groceries like a lifeline. The cracks in the pavement seemed to yawn wider, the shadows stretching longer.

"Write this down," Drumph said once more, his voice breaking through the quiet. "History books are going to study this. They'll study me."

I hit the keys with a dry chuckle, not bothering to meet his gaze. "Got it, chief."

And for the first time, I wasn't sure if I meant it.

I sat back, staring blankly at the screen. The words felt hollow, lifeless. I couldn't help but wonder, what the hell was I doing here? What was the point of all this? It wasn't a memoir—it was a fantasy, a carefully constructed lie, fed to the masses in bite-sized portions.

The irony of it wasn't lost on me. I'd come here to write a book, but all I was doing was chronicling the downfall of reality. My hands had become the tools of his delusion, typing out whatever madness spewed from his mouth. And somehow, people bought it. They always bought it.

What the hell was my purpose in all this? Was I just another cog in the machine, doing my part to prop up the myth? Was that what I was meant for—just sitting here, recording a man's self-destructive climb to the top while I rotted away in his shadow?

Maybe this was it. Maybe this was all I was going to be—another nameless ghost in the background of his empire. Sure, I could walk away. I could quit. But who the hell would care? Who would notice? Hell, maybe that was the real purpose. To witness the collapse from the inside, to be the silent observer, documenting a wrecking ball as it tore through everything in its path.

But even then—wasn't that just another way of running away from the truth? Or maybe I was too deep in it now, too far gone, to even care about what was real anymore.

I thought about the city below—its endless churn, its dark underbelly. The homeless man, gone now, replaced by someone else's story. How long before I became just another nameless face in the crowd, fading into the madness?

For the first time in a long while, I felt a flicker of something. Not hope, but something like it. A nagging thought that maybe, just maybe, there was a way out of this spiral. But how much longer could I take it? How much longer could I sit here and watch this charade unfold, typing out every word, every lie, with no real sense of purpose?

I rubbed my eyes, the weight of it all pressing down on me. I wasn't sure I could keep doing this. I wasn't sure I even wanted to anymore.

chapter: seventeen

The Walk in the Park

It was a crisp fall afternoon in Central Park, the kind of day that practically begged for scarves and steaming cups of cider. The leaves had turned every shade of red, yellow, and orange, and the air carried that undeniable bite of approaching winter. But Drumph, as always, managed to twist the obvious into something uniquely his.

"It's fall, sure," he said, tugging his coat tighter around his chest. "Doesn't it feel warmer? Does it? People say the planet's heating up, but look around. Does this feel warmer to you? It's fall, just like it's always been. Same old fall. Where's this 'global warming' they're all screaming about?"

I shivered under my thin jacket, the cold cutting through me like a knife. It wasn't warm. It was cold, bitterly cold, but Drumph's tone didn't leave room for contradiction. He had that uncanny ability to make you doubt your own senses, to convince you that what you felt—what you knew—wasn't real. This was the man who told you the sky was purple and then had you questioning if you'd ever seen a blue one in the first place.

I stayed silent, but inside, I was shaking my head. "Global warming" is a farce? No, it's not. We're cooking the planet alive, and we all know it, even if we try to ignore it. But Drumph? He was too wrapped up in his self-made bubble of contradictions to see the truth. To him, everything—everything—was part of the scam.

He marched ahead, flanked by his assistant, who carried an unnecessary umbrella, and a bodyguard whose expression hovered somewhere between boredom and existential despair. I trailed behind, notebook in hand, fumbling for the warmth of a lighter. The joint I'd rolled earlier was my only solace in this madness.

"Write this down," Drumph barked, stopping suddenly in the middle of a wide path lined with oak trees. "People need to understand this. It's science. They're always talking about climate change, but look around. Does this look like the end of the world to you? It's beautiful. Perfect. Nature always figures it out. That's what they don't get."

I nodded absently, pen hovering over the page. Drumph's "science" wasn't grounded in any sort of research or reality. It was his twisted version of facts to fit his bloated ego. The same way he had manipulated every bit of media into a form that suited him. The truth didn't matter. The narrative mattered.

"See that?" He pointed at a squirrel digging furiously in the dirt. "That little guy isn't worried about carbon emissions. He's doing his job. Nature adapts. It's fine. They make it sound so complicated, but it's not. It's just common sense. Write that down too."

I scribbled something, trying to capture his latest absurdity, but my mind was elsewhere. This is what happens when people of power, people like Drumph, get their hands on the microphone— they twist everything into a simple, digestible lie. Climate change was real, but the real issue was how few wanted to admit it, especially those with everything to lose. *They're scared, and they're doing everything they can to keep you scared, too.*

"You know, scientists always want to scare you," Drumph continued, oblivious to my thoughts. "They make everything sound worse than it is. You know why? So they can keep their jobs. Scare tactics. It's all a scam. But me? I've always been a scientist. Always."

That was a joke. A man who couldn't spell "science" without asking someone to do it for him, calling himself a scientist. His approach to facts? Pile them on until they look pretty enough to pass for the truth. People bought it, too, like they'd buy a used car with a shiny coat of paint and a broken engine.

"Did you know I predicted the housing bubble? That's science. Patterns. Common sense. They didn't see it coming, but I did. Huge moment. Write that down."

I wasn't sure how much longer I could listen to this. His ability to warp reality was like a magic trick. And the scariest part? *It worked.* People believed him. Hell, *I* almost believed him at times. Maybe that's the true magic trick of it all.

We reached the Bethesda Fountain, where Drumph paused to admire the angel statue at its center. He squinted at it, tilting his head like an art critic evaluating a masterpiece.

"Beautiful, isn't it?" he said. "But you know what would make it better? Gold. Imagine it—gold statues. People would come from all over. It would be incredible. Write that down."

This was the world according to Drumph: an endless cycle of self-aggrandizing ideas, twisted until they fit his narrative. But to *me*, to anyone with eyes, it was a grotesque display of how far removed he was from the world outside his glass tower.

"See that guy?" Drumph said, gesturing vaguely. "He didn't adapt. That's what happens when you let life write your story for you. Me? I write my own story. That's why I'm here, and he's there. Survival of the fittest. Nature."

I exhaled a cloud of smoke, resisting the urge to write what I was really thinking.

"Write this down," Drumph said suddenly, snapping me back to reality. "This is the best chapter. The best one. Make sure they know that."

I nodded, pen in hand. "Got it, chief."

As we walked on, Drumph continued his endless rambling, spewing nonsense that he believed to be gospel. I couldn't stop thinking about what he'd said about nature—about adaptation. If there's one thing I knew, it was that adaptation wasn't about ignoring reality. Adaptation was about *facing* the truth, about dealing with the consequences of our actions. And right now, the truth was that the planet was burning, but Drumph was too busy shining his own gold-plated fantasies to see it.

chapter: eighteen

Velvet Roads and Wasted Kings

Jack. Let's call him Jack. Not because he needed a different name—he's Jack, plain and simple. He's always been Jack. He sat across from me on a battered couch, smoke curling around him like a ghost that wouldn't quit. The kind of guy who lives with one foot in the unreal and the other firmly planted in the wreckage of what's real. A performer by trade, but underneath it all, there's a mind sharp enough to slice through the world's bullshit like a hot knife.

"You ever think about people like them?" Jack asked suddenly, barely moving his lips, his eyes narrowed like he could see through walls. "The ones who fought back. The ones who didn't just bend over for it."

I nodded. The weight of his words hit me hard. Those people—
the ones who fought for something bigger than themselves. They
didn't sell out, didn't turn a blind eye. They left their truth, even
if it only flickered for a moment. Even if they were erased by
history, they still made us see things, feel them, maybe even
change.

"All the time," I said quietly, looking down at my hands,
remembering those figures—those ghosts who'd stood tall in
their own ways. "Especially now. Feels like we need them more
than ever."

Jack took a long drag off his cigarette, his eyes burning through
the walls, as if he could erase them with just his stare. "And
instead, we get Drumph," he spat the name like it was poison on
his tongue. "Feeding the machine. Feeding him. And the worst
part? People eat it up. They line up, tossing cash at him like
they're hoping for a fucking scrap. Pathetic."

"Yeah," I said, lighting my own cigarette, the smoke mingling
with the air between us. "He doesn't just feed on it. He thrives on
it. Every dollar, every cheer, every little nod of approval—it's
like it validates him. Makes him bigger. More."

Jack leaned forward, his eyes narrowing, his voice dropping low
like he was about to make a confession. "You know what's

worse? He believes it. He's not just selling the lie, man. He bought it. Every bit of it. Hook, line, sinker. And the machine keeps turning because we let it. You let it. I let it."

"We all do," I muttered, the bitterness of it all crawling up my throat like bile. "Because it's easier. Because fighting takes courage, and caring takes effort. And people—hell, even me sometimes—we're lazy."

Jack's laugh was hard, sharp, like broken glass. "Lazy? Nah. Lazy would be easy. People aren't lazy. They're scared. That's the problem. Terrified of what happens if they look up, really look, and see the truth—see how bad it is. So they keep their heads down, hands moving, and they keep feeding the fucking thing."

"It's survival," I said, but the words tasted bitter, like they didn't belong to me anymore. "People are just trying to get by. And he knows it. He exploits it."

Jack's eyes locked on mine like he was trying to peel back every layer of myself that I didn't want to show. "And you? What the hell are you doing there?"

"Every damn day," I said, exhaling a plume of smoke, the question hitting me harder than I expected. "I'm trying to figure it out."

Jack shook his head slowly, as if this was just another show he'd already seen a thousand times. "You're feeding him. Every word you write, every page you turn, every chapter—it's all fuel. You're not just keeping the machine running, man—you're throwing logs on the fire."

I felt the sting, but there was truth in it. The kind of truth you don't want to face. The truth that burns.

"You ever think about what those people would say if they were here?" Jack asked, his voice quieter now, but still cutting. "What they'd write?"

I took a long drag, watching the smoke twist and dance in the air. "Yeah. They'd probably tell us to grab a fistful of courage and burn it all to the ground."

Jack shook his head with a faint smile. "Nah. They wouldn't burn it all down. That's the easy way. They'd tell us to build something better. Because burning it down? Anyone can do that. The hard part is creating something worth keeping."

I stared at him, really stared. And for a moment, I saw more in him than I expected: the pain, the frustration, the fear. And underneath it all, a flicker of hope, as if he wasn't ready to quit just yet. And I realized, he was right. Again.

"The thing about people like that," I said slowly, "is they don't just tell the truth. They make you feel it. They make you see it in a way you can't unsee. That's why they're dangerous. That's why they matter. Because once you see the truth, you can't ignore it. And that's what scares people like Drumph. That's why they hate artists. Because artists make people care."

And I turned back to the typewriter, my fingers hovering over the keys. The world outside was still dark, broken—twisted with greed, apathy, and cruelty. But maybe, just maybe, there was still hope. Maybe there were still people out there who cared enough to fight, to create, to make people care.

And maybe, if I did it right, this book could be part of that fight.

Jack's voice broke through my fog of thoughts. "You look like hell, man."

I glanced over at him, slouched on the couch with a cigarette dangling lazily from his lips. "Feel like it too," I said, my voice flat.

"Why do you keep doing this to yourself?" he asked, gesturing at the typewriter, dismissive but knowing. "You're not a kid anymore. Nobody's expecting you to save the world."

I stared at the blank page, the cursor blinking like a mocking heartbeat. "I don't know. Maybe it's just easier to keep punching at the machine than sit back and watch it crush everything."

Jack snorted, his lips curling into a bitter smile. "Has punching the machine ever worked? Look around. People don't want to be saved anymore. They're too comfortable, too scared, or too damn tired to care. You could write the most brilliant thing in the world, and it wouldn't make a dent."

"Then what the hell are we doing here?" I snapped, the frustration seeping out. "What's the point of any of this if it's all so hopeless?"

Jack paused. He took a long drag, his eyes flicking over to the window as though searching for something he couldn't quite articulate. The smoke lingered in the air, like his thoughts. "Yeah, but it's not about saving the world. Never has been. It's about saving pieces of it. One person, one moment at a time. There's people out there. Not groups. Not Rebs, or Dems, or Libs, or whatever the hell they wanna call themselves these days. They're just people. And yeah, they've gotten lost. Political preferences are like a race to them now—get a label, pick a side, forget the rest. But there's people, real ones. I don't care about numbers, about a movement. We're entertainers, man. We speak to people, not the groups, but to them, the individuals. That's the point. Not a number. A connection. Big or small. If for nothing else, for just one second, we give 'em a reason to smile as the machine grinds on. A smile not born from some ignorant bliss, but from a moment of clarity. They get it for a minute, even if it's just a second."

I sat there, lost in my thoughts, staring at the reflection of the city lights flickering outside the window. I caught a glimpse of myself in the mirror, the lines of my face older than I remembered. What little hair was left, thinning and greying, sideburns more wild than anything close to neat. The weight— more than just physical—settled deep into my bones. It wasn't just from the years, the decisions I'd made, or the mess I kept making. No, it was something else. The weight of it all. I didn't regret any of it, not really. After all, life was supposed to be one hell of a ride, and damn, it sure had been.

But that gnawing pain, both physical and mental, a constant hum that wouldn't go away, had me wondering: Maybe I don't get it. Maybe I never did. Maybe Drumph is right.

The thought hung there, like smoke from a cigarette I never smoked. The sharp tinge of doubt crept in, the kind that makes you question everything you've believed in, everything you've fought for. What if we're all just full of shit? What if this whole fight, this push against the system, was just a performance? Something to distract us from the bigger truth? A joke we couldn't see, because we were too busy laughing at the wrong things.

I glanced at Jack. He had stopped talking, probably noticed my head was somewhere else. He didn't press. But the weight of it kept pushing down on me. That gnawing doubt. What if all of this—the fight, the words, the pain—meant nothing? What if, despite everything, Drumph's way was the one that worked? What if he was right?

I shook my head, fighting the thoughts, but they clung to me like shadows.

"You ever think about him?" I asked suddenly, turning to Jack. His expression remained steady, but I could see the glint of curiosity in his eyes. "Drumph. Do you ever wonder what he'd be without all this?"

Jack blinked, the question hanging in the air for a moment. I could tell he wasn't sure where I was going with it, but he waited.

I leaned forward, the weight of the question pressing on me. "What if he's right? What if he's the one who actually gets it? What if we're all just chasing ghosts, trying to play the game when he already owns the board?"

Jack took a long drag, his eyes narrowing slightly, though not out of judgment. More like he was trying to see through the haze of doubt I had spun around myself. He didn't answer immediately, his gaze far off, lost somewhere between the flickering city lights outside and the smoke in his hand.

Then, he spoke, slow and deliberate, his words feeling like a punch to the gut. "You know," Jack said, leaning forward, "it's not about getting it. It's about seeing the damn thing for what it is. The thing about Drumph is, he doesn't see it. He's just one of the players in the game, but he thinks he's the whole damn system. He's the problem, man. Not the answer."

I stayed silent, trying to process what he was saying. The noise in my head quieted for a second, enough for me to think clearly. Jack was right, I think. At least, for now, in this moment. I wasn't sure what was real anymore, but I was damn sure Drumph's brand of reality wasn't going to be the one that saved us.

Jack took another drag, the smoke escaping his mouth like a cloud around the truth we were both trying to understand. "Maybe we don't need to get it, man. Maybe we just need to keep pushing. Keep asking questions. Sure, we're all full of doubt. We all wonder if any of it matters. But we can't let that stop us from pushing forward, because if we do, then we might as well be like him. Just sitting on the throne of bullshit, pretending everything's fine."

I let that sink in for a moment, the weight of Jack's words pressing down on me again. Yeah, I thought. Maybe we'll never really "get it." But maybe it's not about getting it. Maybe it's about not letting the bullshit drown us out. Even if the ride is broken, at least we're still on it. And that's something.

chapter: nineteen

The Ride Continues

I was flying east, hurtling through the dark skies from Los Angeles back to New York. The plane hummed beneath me, a quiet monotone that blurred into the static of my thoughts. A laptop sat open on the tray table in front of me, its screen glowing faintly in the dim cabin light. The glass of whiskey at my elbow had grown warm, untouched since takeoff.

I stared at the blinking cursor on the screen, its rhythmic pulse both mocking and hypnotic. The words wouldn't come—not here, not now. Not after the last week spent mired in the unholy glow of Los Angeles, the city where everything shines but nothing illuminates.

The cabin was quiet, save for the occasional clink of glasses or the hushed murmur of a flight attendant offering refills. I shifted uncomfortably in my seat, the ache in my back a constant reminder of years hunched over typewriters and computers. Creation, they call it, this thing we do. But sometimes, it feels more like excavation—digging through layers of bullshit and exhaustion to find some kernel of truth worth exposing.

I glanced out the window, the endless void of the night sky reflecting back at me. It was a fitting backdrop for the thoughts swirling in my head, the ones I couldn't escape no matter how far I flew. Politics, culture, greed, despair—the toxic stew of a society in freefall.

Football season is over. The phrase rattled around in my mind like a loose coin in a tin can. It had once been a joke, a dark quip about the futility of it all. But now, it felt more like a grim prophecy. The game was over, the field abandoned, the scoreboard forgotten. What was left was something far worse—a theater of endless spectacle, where the players were replaced by puppets and the audience was too numb to notice.

Politics. A carnival of greed and treachery, as I'd once written. The democratic process had devolved into a grotesque parody of itself, a puppet show where the strings were pulled by corporate money and the media's insatiable hunger for scandal. The voters? Just extras in the background, their apathy and desperation the fuel that kept the whole machine running. It wasn't governance—it was a performance, and a bad one at that.

Culture. The algorithms had seen to that. Social media had turned us into tribes of screeching chimps, throwing rocks at shadows and calling it justice. The echo chambers were perfect, airtight. No dissent, no debate, just a constant loop of affirmation and outrage. Critical thinking was dead, replaced by the comforting hum of confirmation bias. The "season" of meaningful cultural exchange had been over for years, though most hadn't noticed—or cared.

And then there was the economy. Corporate greed had metastasized into something monstrous, a beast that devoured everything in its path. Climate change, economic inequality, healthcare—none of it mattered as long as the stock prices stayed high and the bonuses kept flowing. It was a game, rigged from the start, and the referees had long since been bought off.

But the worst of it? The apathy. The sheer, suffocating apathy. People were tired, beaten down by a relentless onslaught of crises and chaos. They'd stopped fighting, stopped caring. The fight was over before it had even begun. Football season is over.

The flight attendant appeared at my elbow, offering a refill. I nodded, and she poured the amber liquid into my glass with practiced precision. As she walked away, I caught a glimpse of the magazine tucked under her arm—a glossy cover featuring Drumph's smirking face, the headline screaming some inane proclamation of his greatness.

Drumph. The man I was flying back to write for. The man who epitomized everything wrong with this twisted, broken world. He wasn't a man, not really. He was a brand, a hollow shell filled with greed and bombast. A vacuum that sucked in everything around him and spat out more emptiness. And the worst part? People worshipped it. They saw the hollow and called it whole.

But for a second, I wondered—who the hell made him this way? Who turned him into this bloated caricature of a man, standing at the center of this circus, wearing the mask of confidence when inside he was just another pawn? The system. The machine. Maybe Drumph wasn't the problem at all. Maybe he was just a cog, another cog that had been chewed up and spit out by a system that had been grinding away for decades. It wasn't like he woke up one day with the goal of tearing everything down—no, he genuinely believed in his own version of success. He thought he was helping. He was the product of it all—the media, the money, the lies. He didn't just get there by chance. He'd played the game well. His name, once synonymous with New York's skyline, now reverberated in tabloids and on the lips of people who dreamed of more than they could ever have. Reality TV had made him a household name, a symbol of wealth and ambition.

His casinos, his real estate empire, they were all part of the same glittering illusion. People followed him because they saw him as a success story—a self-made man. But they didn't see the cracks. The bankruptcies. The failed ventures. The scandals. All they saw was the empire. All they heard was the success.

He was a symbol of the American dream, or at least the version people had bought into. Hell, it was easy to follow someone like him. He was larger than life, a walking advertisement for wealth, power, and success. He made people believe that if they just worked hard enough, they could be him. That's what they bought. That's what they wanted. The idea that there was a shortcut to greatness. A fast lane to riches. But what were they really following? A man who had leveraged his name and image into a multi-million-dollar empire, but who had spent his entire career teetering on the edge of bankruptcy, constantly restructuring to keep his head above water. It wasn't about honesty. It was about perception.

I shook my head, trying to push the thought away. Because no matter how I sliced it, Drumph was still the one standing on top, shoveling the shit onto the world and getting away with it. He wasn't a victim of the system—he was just a symptom of it. A loud, obnoxious, hollow symptom that everyone latched onto, giving him the power he didn't deserve.

I took another sip of whiskey, the burn of it settling somewhere deep in my chest. That was the real game, wasn't it? Not just exposing the lies, but questioning what made them so powerful. Who were the real puppeteers? Who pulled the strings while we focused on the puppet? I wasn't so sure anymore, but I knew this much: it wasn't going to end just by getting rid of Drumph.

Buy the ticket. Take the ride. The phrase slipped into my mind like an old friend, a reminder of what it had all been about in the beginning. The chaos, the rebellion, the refusal to go quietly into the night. The fight might have been hopeless, but that didn't mean it wasn't worth fighting.

I cracked my knuckles, took another sip of whiskey, and started to type. The words crawled out of me, heavy and deliberate, carving themselves into the blank void of the screen. Somewhere outside the cabin, the first light of dawn began to creep over the horizon. A new day, for whatever it was worth.

The ride was still going, whether I liked it or not. And so, I wrote.

chapter: twenty

The Most Important Chapter

Drumph paced the office, muttering to himself as the hum of the air conditioning blended with the clink of his shoes on the marble floor. Each step echoed off the golden walls, a reminder of the gilded cage he'd built for himself. "This is it," he said, stopping abruptly and pointing to the ceiling as if the answer had been there all along, just waiting to be revealed. "This is the most important chapter. The one they'll quote in schools. They'll teach this, you know. Like Lincoln. Like Churchill."

I leaned back in my chair, the soft hum of the laptop ticking in the background, my eyes tracing the screen's faint glow. The golden monstrosity he'd insisted I use sat untouched in the corner like a forgotten trophy. I wasn't going to touch it. Not now. Not ever.

"Write this down," Drumph barked, his voice snapping through the stillness. "We're talking about politics first. The truth about me—the outsider. The disruptor. The guy who came in and broke all their little rules because the rules were rigged."

I pressed a key idly, letting the cursor blink in rhythm with the silence. "Go on."

"They said it couldn't be done," he continued, his voice rising with indignation. "But I did it. I took on the corrupt establishment. The real estate elites, the politicians—they all wanted me gone. But I showed them. I built an empire. I created jobs. I made New York great again."

I stared at the screen, my fingers hovering over the keys. *What am I doing?* I thought. *Feeding this nonsense? Writing his gospel?* Drumph wasn't fighting the system. He was feeding it, bloating himself on the same parasitic structure that had crushed everyone else under its heel. He wasn't the problem—he was a symptom. But, *wasn't I too?*

I typed: *Politics is not a game. It's not a spectacle. When truth dies, power wins.*

Drumph didn't notice. He was already spinning onto the next subject, like a carnival barker moving to the next illusion.

"Culture," he said, waving his arms dramatically. "They call me divisive. Me! But I'm the one who fights against the phonies, the pretenders. I've built a brand that's real. People respect that. That's why they come to my buildings, buy my products, watch my shows. They want the real deal. They want Drumph."

I glanced at the muted television in the corner of the room, where reruns of *The Apprentice* flickered—a parade of contestants fighting tooth and nail for his approval under the harsh lights of a conference room. *Not culture*, I thought. *Chaos.* A twisted competition where nothing real was born, just hollow spectacles for consumption.

I typed: *Culture is dead when the loudest voices drown out the truest ones. When screens divide instead of connect, when outrage replaces thought, we lose the thread of humanity.*

"Corporate greed," Drumph said, his voice unyielding. "They say I'm the problem, but I'm the solution. I've shown people how to win. Look at my casinos. My buildings. My deals. I've brought money into places where there wasn't any. I've created opportunity. And let's be honest—America loves a winner."

I bit my tongue, suppressing the laugh that threatened to spill out. *America loves money*, I thought. Drumph had perfected the art of turning everything into a commodity, including failure. People, ideas, even his own shortcomings—everything was just a product to sell.

I typed: *Greed is not growth. Wealth is not wisdom. A system that rewards exploitation is not a system worth saving.*

Drumph stopped pacing, a gleam of satisfaction lighting up his eyes. "Are you getting this? This is good stuff. Real good stuff."

"Every word," I lied, tapping the keys with the practiced rhythm of a man who had long since ceased believing his own bullshit.

"Apathy," he said, his voice dropping, now tinged with faux solemnity. "That's what they don't get. I woke people up. I gave them something to believe in. Before me, they were hopeless, broken. Now? Now they have pride. They have purpose."

I looked at him, his self-congratulatory flush a stark contrast to the hollow man I had come to know. *Hopelessness wasn't his enemy—it was his fuel.* He thrived on it, packaged it as hope, and sold it back to the masses who had grown too tired to question it.

I typed: *Despair isn't an excuse. It's a call to arms. The moment we stop fighting, the moment we stop caring, the machine wins.*

Drumph's voice thundered again. "And then there's the lies. They say I lie! Can you believe it? I'm the most honest guy you'll ever meet. A truth-teller. A counter-puncher. That's why they hate me, because I tell it like it is."

I typed: *When words lose meaning, truth loses power. The loudest liar doesn't win. We lose.*

Drumph leaned over my shoulder suddenly, squinting at the screen, his expression morphing into confusion, then rage. "What the fuck is this?" he shouted, slamming his hand down on the desk. "This isn't what I said!"

"It's what you meant," I said calmly, not looking up.

"Delete it!" he roared, his face turning an unhealthy shade of red. "Delete all of it and write what I said! Exactly what I said!"

I didn't move. Slowly, deliberately, I hit the backspace key, erasing the lines one by one. But not from my files. Not really.

Drumph straightened himself up, smoothing his tie like a boxer who had just finished throwing a tantrum. "Good. Now write this: Obama is the worst thing to happen to this country. He's not even American. He's trying to destroy everything we stand for."

I didn't type.

"Did you hear me?" Drumph demanded. "Write it down! This is the most important part of the book. History will remember this."

I typed: *Obama has different views that don't align with mine, but that doesn't mean he's trying to destroy America.*

Drumph's face contorted with fury, his voice growing dangerously loud. "No! That's not what I said! Delete it and write the truth!"

I didn't move.

He leaned in closer, his breath hot and acrid. "You're fired. You hear me? Fired!"

I stood, closing my laptop and slinging my bag over my shoulder. "Don't hire a demolitionist to build a castle," I said, a cold certainty settling in. "You made a bad choice."

As I turned to leave, the door opened, and Melodia stepped in. She glanced at me with that unreadable expression, then offered a faint smile. Almost imperceptibly, she winked.

Drumph's voice followed me down the hallway, his petulant roar echoing through the golden labyrinth. "You're fired! You'll never work in this town again!"

I didn't look back. The ride was over.

The elevator descended slowly, each floor a quiet countdown. My back pressed against the cold, steel walls as the hum of the ride filled the air. The security guard beside me stood still, his eyes fixed on the doors, as if he'd seen this before. And maybe he had. Maybe this wasn't the first time someone had walked out of that office, unsure if they'd just lost or if they'd finally seen it for what it was.

But this—this felt different. This wasn't a defeat. It wasn't about winning or losing anymore. I was starting to get it.

I wasn't just rejecting Drumph. I wasn't rejecting the fight because it felt too big, too messy, too hopeless. No, this wasn't a resignation. This was the realization that the fight itself—the fight for who's right, who's wrong, who's worthy—was the problem.

It's not about what's right. It's not about proving a point, tearing down the others, or even holding up a mirror to a corrupt system. It's all part of the same damn cycle. It's all part of the machine. Whether it was Drumph, or me, or anyone else on the other side, the fight was just feeding it.

For a moment, I questioned myself. I wasn't sure if I was still playing into the same damn thing by walking away, by stepping off the track. Wasn't I still trying to control the outcome? Wasn't I still trying to make the right choice, the "righteous" choice?

That was the trap. I had been fighting because I wanted to be right. I had wanted to prove something—not just to him, but to myself, to the world. I thought that's what mattered. But what if I was just feeding the very thing I was trying to defeat?

I looked at the numbers tick by, floor by floor. Each one felt like a tick off the clock, the time I had spent in this game. The truth was painful, but it was also freeing. Stepping away wasn't surrendering—it was choosing to stop feeding the machine.

The fight wasn't about winning. It wasn't about fighting for some greater purpose anymore. It wasn't about being right, proving a point. The fight, in any form, was just the game. And the game would keep going as long as we all kept playing.

The doors opened with a soft whoosh, and the sterile light of the lobby spilled in. I stepped out, nodding to the guard, but I didn't stop. I kept walking, not because I had given up, but because I was finally making the choice not to play.

Was that the end of it? Would the machine stop turning without me? Probably not. But maybe, just maybe, I was done with trying to fix it by playing the same damn game.

Maybe stepping off the track was the only way to change anything. Not by winning. Not by fighting. But by refusing to feed the cycle.

*The only honest exit is to **wake from the hallucination.***

www.ingramcontent.com/pod-product-compliance
Lightning Source LLC
Chambersburg PA
CBHW072027170626
46811CB00008B/2973